# PRIDE'S RUN

## CATHRYN FOX WRITING AS CAT KALEN

Discover other titles by Cathryn Fox at www.cathrynfox.com. Please sign up for Cathryn's Newsletter for freebies, ebooks, news and contests:

https://app.mailerlite.com/webforms/landing/c1f8n1

ISBN 978-0-9878559-1-6
ISBN Print 978-0-9878559-0-9

*For Allison*

$$1$$

*California Wine Country*
       *August 23^{rd}, six days until full moon*

**The** click of the lock at the top of the stairwell is my only indication that morning is upon me. My ears perk up and I listen for the coming footfalls. The weight on the stairs combined with the creaking of each wooden step will let me know which handler has come for us this time, which unlucky puppet has drawn the short straw and is stuck with letting the dogs out, or in this case, the werewolves.

Sure, he'll come sauntering down the stairs sporting a brave face and looking at me with cold, dark eyes meant to intimidate. But the wolf inside me can smell his inner fear. Despite the fact that I'm the one caged, underneath the handler's cool, superficial shell he's the one who's truly afraid.

A long column of light filters down the stairs and I blink my eyes into focus as the bright rays infiltrate the pitch black cellar. I don't really need to blink. Not with my exceptional vision. But I do it anyway because sometimes I simply like to pretend I'm a normal seventeen-year-old girl, one who can't see in the dark. It's nonsense, I know. I'm not fooling anyone. Least of all myself.

The door yawns wider and before the first heavy boot, soiled with old blood that he'll pass off as wine stains, hits the top step, my senses go on high alert. I never know what morning will bring—or who will bring it.

A breeze rushes down the stairs ahead of the handler, carrying the aroma of the grand estate with it. I push past the metallic scent of dried blood to catch traces of grape juice in the air, a common smell on the majestic vineyard—that and illegal drugs, the estate's real source of income. Going beyond those familiar fragrances, I breathe deeper and get hints of fresh bread baking in the upstairs kitchen. It must be Thursday. Mica, the estate's cook, always bakes on Thursday.

In my human form I roll onto my side and lean toward the smell. Wistfully, my tongue darts out and brushes over my bottom lip. There is something about that scent that always entices me and before I can help it I envision myself eating a warm slice covered in rich creamy butter, crispy on the outside, moist and tender on the inside.

My nostrils widen, but I know the bread isn't meant for me and not even one delicious crumb will pass over my dry lips. Not unless Mica sneaks it to me. As much as I'd love to taste her offerings I don't like it when she takes chances for me. Disobedience is far too risky for the aging housekeeper. Despite that, my stomach growls in response to the aroma and I fight off the cravings. I can't hope for bread when it's unlikely that I'll even be given a scrap of food today, especially if I can't please him.

My master.

A boot hits the second step—the handlers always descend slowly—and as I stretch my legs out on my dusty mattress I hear the waking groans of Jace and Clover stirring in their own cages beside me. I glance their way, and that's when my attention falls on the one empty cage in the cellar. My mother's den. I breathe deep and fight off a pang of sadness that I cannot afford to feel.

I turn away from the empty cage and stare at the gray cement walls. I can't bear to look at her den any longer. It only reminds me of how they killed her and how all the pups were forced to watch—to learn that disobedience comes with a price. Guilt and sorrow eat at me to think that she'd died trying to free me.

When step number five creaks, I diligently try to shake off the memories. The handler is close which means I can't think about my mother right now. I push all thoughts of her aside, knowing that right now I have to think about my father and what he taught me before the master killed him. Never let them see your fear.

I harden myself.

Prepare.

Before my master's puppet even reaches the bottom step, I know it's the one they call Lawrence, the handler I hate the most. The one with a weak mind, strong back, teeth like baked beans and beady eyes that fit his ugly rat face.

He likes to call me kitten. I have a few choice names that I'd like to call him in return, but I always bite the inside of my cheek to resist the urge. Partly because I'd be whipped and partly because Miss Kara educated me and taught me all about manners. I realize that an educated wolf with manners might sound laughable. In my line of work, however, education and manners are as lethal as a bear trap to those I hunt. That's how I lure my marks, how I bait my prey. A pretty face and good grace go a long way for a trained killer like me.

My glance wanders to my leg, the one peeking out from beneath my ratty blanket, and my eyes are drawn to the long jagged scar tracking the length of my calf. I grimace. Even with my education and manners, I never forget what I really am. I'm never allowed to.

"Hey kitten," Lawrence says. Most would think the nickname is a play on my birth name, Pride. But I know it's the handler's way of cutting me down, to find control where he feels none. My parents called me Pride because I was their pride and joy. Lions live in a pride and since lions are cats...

He tosses a collar and chain into my cage. "Leash up."

I take note of the gun in his holster before my glance locks on his. As I give him a good hard stare, he flinches. The movement is slight, but I notice it. Dressed in my knee length nightgown, long hair loose around my shoulders, I might look like an average seventeen-year-old girl—harmless and innocent—but we all know I'm not.

Even though Lawrence keeps his face blank and stares down at me with those dark eyes of his, he reeks of terror. The scent is like a mixture of hot sweat and rotting compost. Oh, it's not pretty by any means. Nevertheless, the werewolf slumbering restlessly inside me feeds off his fear, thrives on it, so I inhale and draw it deep into my lungs.

Without taking my eyes off his, I take my time to leash up. My movements are slow and deliberate as I position the collar. Metal grinds metal and the sound cuts the silence as I secure it around my neck. The handler winces. So do the older, more obedient wolves that I bunk with.

Jace cuts me a glance, chocolate eyes now milky from old age warn me to behave. I realize he's doing it for my own good, but this morning I'm cold and hungry and in no mood for Lawrence's insults. Clover makes a noise to draw the handler's attention away from me, and all sets of eyes shift to her.

As Clover tries to pacify Lawrence, averting her gaze in a show of respect and making small talk about the weather,

Lawrence opens my mother's former cage and pulls out her cot. He gives it a good hard shake and the breeze stirs the dust on the unfinished boards masquerading as our ceiling. The particles dance in the stairwell light before falling to the cold, cement floor.

When Lawrence tosses the cot into a corner I stiffen. It can only mean one thing. My mother has been gone for a little over a year now, and I know the master rarely keeps a cell empty for long, which makes me wonder when and how he's going to fill it?

Who will he breed?

I cringe at the thought of bringing puppies into this world, but know it's not something I have to worry about. The master would never breed a wolf like me. My mother always said I was a survivor, the only pup in a litter of three to make it, but hey, a runt is a runt. Thanks to Darwin and his theory of 'natural selection' a runt is a heritable trait that a pack can do without. When it comes to canine reproduction, only one motto dictates: runts need not apply.

Deep in the bowels of the estate's basement, the master keeps other wolves, separating the strong and young from one another. I'm smart enough to understand that he distances us so we can't conspire against him or speak telepathically. Wolves can only use telepathy when in animal form, however. Well, most wolves that is. Oddly enough, I along with Stone, an alpha wolf two years my senior, are able to communicate while in our human forms.

Sometimes the master does in-house breeding, sometimes he sends us out to one of his associates—other drug lords who also harbor werewolves. It's like he's running a regular old puppy mill in here. Except his puppies kill for him. Which begs the question, what does my master have in store for me today?

2

At the top of the stairs I hear the master bark out an order to one of his other handlers. Lawrence's fingers quiver in response as he slides his key into the padlock securing my cell, a clear indication that the wolves aren't the only ones afraid of their keeper. I look past his shoulder, at the streak of light filtering downward and illuminating a path to the grand mansion up above.

"Going somewhere?" he taunts. I glare at him and his expressionless mask shatters for a brief moment. He offers me a smug smile, but I hear the slight tremor when he exhales.

I make a noise, a mixture of a human moan and an animal growl, and his hand slows on my lock. Escape from the compound might be impossible, but it doesn't mean I don't think about it. I like to exercise my mind by trying to find holes in the security system. Most would think I'm simply daydreaming but what I'm really doing is watching, listening, learning and absorbing everything about the estate and the people who run it.

The compound is huge and so far I'm unable to figure out

a way to get through the electric fence. Even if I do overcome that first obstacle and make it to the other side, I can't forget about that pesky microchip beneath my skin, a tiny transponder with a permanent radio-frequency identification.

I could try to run while out on a job, like my mother did. But capture came swift for her as she tried to make her way toward the Canadian border, to where she believed wolves ran free. I'm not sure if that's true or not, or even if those packs would have helped her break the rest of us out if she'd found them.

As I think about escape I wonder how far I would get before another tracker found me. Or would the Paranormal Task Force—an elite group of officers who hunt things that go bump in the night—catch me first?

The hinges on my cell groan like a wounded animal as Lawrence pulls open the door and makes a grab for my chain. I know better than to shift to my primal form with the collar on. One of the pups broke his neck that way. Another lesson compliments of our master.

Lawrence yanks on the chain and jerks me to my feet as his gaze rakes over my dusty floor. With that grin still on his ugly rat face, he uses his stained boot to brush away the picture I drew in the thin layer of dirt.

I won't let him see me flinch, I won't give him that power, so I clench my jaw hard enough to grind bone and resist the urge to kill him.

It's a silly thing, really, but I hate how he takes pleasure in erasing the one thing that gives me joy. Drawing. I once saw the master's wife—I think it was his third wife—using water colors to paint a picture of the vineyard and I thought it was the most beautiful thing I'd ever seen.

I stretch my leg muscles as I exit my cage and wait for him to release Jace and Clover. Then, with three chains in his hand, Lawrence leads us all up the stairwell. The windows are open and a warm breeze blows over my flesh, rustling the hem of my nightgown.

He herds us down a long walkway until we reach the kitchen. I keep my head down as I walk past Mica, not because she looks at me with pity, she doesn't, but because I don't want her to see my wolf's hunger. Hunger for her bread.

Hunger for her blood.

Like every other morning we leave the kitchen and step out into the vast outdoors and prepare for our daily run and agility training. With the warm, sun-kissed grass tickling my bare feet I stand there for a moment and inhale the bouquet. The master's estate is on the west coast, smack dab in the middle of wine country, and if I listen really hard, way off in the distance I can almost hear the Pacific waters lapping lazily against the sandy shoreline. My ears perk as I listen to the soothing sound. Something about the translucent blue ocean with its rolling surf and unpredictable waves reminds me of freedom, but now is not the time to be thinking about such things. It's time to be thinking about captivity and what that means for me.

As I stand there absorbing the new day, and the familiarity of it all, I don't take pleasure in the aromatic smells from the juicy berries blossoming beneath the late summer sun, like some of the other shifters around me do. Instead I study my surroundings. Survival instincts force me to look for a change, to check and see if anything has been altered.

I stretch out my limbs as I once again commit the courtyard to memory, glancing at the extreme obstacle course and noting the additions that now make it that much more challenging. We have everything from ropes, walls, hurdles, zigzags, tunnels/low rails, fences, cargo net climbs, cargo net descents and parallel bars. Every obstacle is designed to test and increase our endurance, speed, ability and balance.

I take my time to glare at the men looking down at the

dozen shifters walking the yard. From their perch, high on top of a sturdy brick wall surrounding the courtyard, they keep us in line. Same as always, six men, guns aimed and ready to shoot should we try to escape, not that escape from the yard is an option. Not with four huge walls confining us. It's impossible I know, but like I said, it still doesn't stop me from thinking about it.

On a distant hill a propane-fired cannon blasts and loud squawking follows. The cannon is used to startle the birds and scare them away from the vineyard's berries.

The other wolves have gotten so used to the sound they barely register it. I, on the other hand, like to count the minutes in between each detonation because I can't help thinking that maybe someday I'll be able to use the noise to my advantage.

I turn my focus back to the immediate task before me, and like the others, I begin to strip. Modesty is a privilege we're not gifted with and something I've gotten used to over the years. As the runt of the family, I still have the body of a twelve year old, boy—flat and gangly in all the wrong places.

Naked beneath the glaring sun, I fold my nightgown carefully and place it on the grass near the house. Oddly enough, taking care of my belongings gives me a sense of normalcy in a world where none exists.

I look over the grounds and stare at the other, mature wolves. A half a dozen or so puppies are still inside, coddling in their nurseries. My heart squeezes as I remember those days. But I quickly tamp down those feelings and focus on the others.

Who will the master pit me against today?

My glance settles on Stone, who, like me, was born in the compound. I'm not sure why there is telepathy between us when we're in our human forms, or what it could mean. All I know is that it defies our nature and isn't something either of us wants anyone to know.

At nineteen, Stone has grown into a powerful, dominating alpha. It was only a few years ago, right around his sixteenth birthday, when the master finally broke him. I'm not sure what it took. No one is, really. But we do know that Stone is a bit of a wild card. Ever since the master gained control of his wolf, Stone has become increasingly aggressive toward me, forcing me to block him from my thoughts. I have no interest in communicating with him now, in wolf or in human form.

Our eyes meet across the yard and his ruthless silver orbs glare back at me. I used to wonder if his parents named him Stone because he was as dense as one. I don't wonder any more.

Stone doesn't like that my brains match his brawn, and I don't like his rumors that I'm 'doing it' with the master for extra food. Extra food feeds the brain, but that's not why I'm smart. I'm smart because of my breeding. And lessons learned have taught me that someone of my size needs to fight with their head, not their heart.

A high-pitched yelp pierces the air and I tear my gaze from Stone's. I spin around in time to see the master's leather strap slice open Sandy's back—a young wolf named for the color of her fur. Rivulets of crimson trickle down her peachy flesh and spill across the grass, turning it a coppery shade of red. Like an air freshener, the sweet scent of warm blood catches on a breeze and fans out. Soft, hungry growls sound in response.

My fingers curl into fists and the taste of blood fills my mouth as I bite the inside of my cheek. Guilt that I'm unable to help her—that I'd been unable to help my parents—churns inside me and I hate how powerless I feel.

My mind races as I take another quick glance around the courtyard. There has to be a way to break free from the master's control. I'm convinced of it. I just have to figure out what it is. That thought always helps me pull myself together and gives me a seed of hope.

The master barks out an order and cuts the air with his strap. Sandy is a pup, a few years younger than me and she hasn't learned to play the game yet, hasn't learned when to push and when to back off. My nostrils flare and I try not to react, to show emotions as the deafening snap of the strap punctures the barriers shielding my emotions. I refuse to let anyone see a sign of weakness in me.

When she continues to whimper, my stomach lurches, and I want to vomit, except there is nothing inside my gut to bring up. The violent impulse to kill twists my insides. I should help her. I want to help her. In fact, I want to tear the master's head clear off his neck and feed it to the wolves. Instead, I desensitize. It's the only way I can get through another day. But it doesn't stop me from stealing a look at the bulging purple mark tracking my leg. We might have regenerative abilities, able to heal ourselves and close our own wounds, but the scars always remain, inside and out.

Her whimpering stops and the master leaves her. I look at her but she doesn't return my gaze. She reaches for him. *Him.* Her thin fingers wiggling like underfed worms, begging for forgiveness and approval, but he turns his back on her, discarding her like she is nothing more than yesterday's puppy-soaked newspaper. It's a form of punishment, a proven way to train and break a pup. Most of the wolves want to please him after they've been broken. I'm not one of them.

I won't be broken.

The master, of course, insists he's doing us wolves a favor by confining us and likes to point out that he keeps us alive, protected from the PTF, and allows us to feed on the one thing we love most.

Humans.

I still wonder how he found out about us, and how he was able to first trap the elders. Rumor has it that his second wife was killed by a wolf and he'd witnessed it. Then he went hunting, not to kill us, but to use us.

Key in hand, Mario, one of the three handlers in the courtyard, comes by to remove my collar. With cognac-toned skin, his dark hair is long and tied into a ponytail that reaches the middle of his back. I put him around his mid thirties. Unlike Lawrence, Mario is always nice to me, but he's still one of them and I never let myself forget it.

"You're up against Stone today," he says and looks at me, his glance avoiding my eyes. "You both go first."

I nod, and then something flickers in his eyes when he sees the way my pale, stringy flesh stretches taught over my protruding ribs. I let him look and don't try to make it easy for him. If they all hate what he does to us so much, why don't they do something about it? I don't ask. I already know the answer to that question. They can't.

I once heard a few staff members whispering about illegal immigrants. During one of my manner lessons I asked Miss Kara what it meant. Instead of answering, she paled and darted to the bathroom. I took that opportunity to do a quick search on her computer, and what I found sickened me.

The master likes to collect people in much the same manner as he collects animals. His entire staff is made up of these immigrants, men and women who've come to this country looking for a better life. Should any of them question his orders punishment would, undoubtedly, come in the form of deportation. Or perhaps even worse.

As my mood darkens, clouds move across the sky, eclipsing the summer sun and giving us a break from the dry heat.

"Have you looked over the course?" he whispers quietly, his dark eyes darting around nervously.

I know what he's talking about, and I know he's taking a risk in even hinting at it, but I don't respond. Instead, I turn my focus to the master who commands the attention of all those around him as he moves through the imprisoned court-yard, examining his pets. Since I'd like to eat today, I use that time to gather myself and get my head into the game. It will take all my intelligence and concentration to match Stone's strength.

Bones crack in protest when I turn my head from side to side, stretching my neck. As I call on my wolf, the pain of the shift pulls at me and I focus on it fully, using it to fuel my blood and power my body.

Shifting is never easy, and while our wolf is ruled by the moon, we can morph anytime we like. I usually only trans-form when forced, like during our training sessions or when the master demands I make a kill. During the full moon, however, we have no choice but to shift. There is nothing we can do to fight the power it has over us.

My body begins to shake, air rushes from my lungs. Unsta-ble, I drop to the ground. Landing on all fours, my flesh stretches, tears, and my bones elongate. Blood burns in my veins as my wolf claws its way out of my young, human body. A moment later I feel the warm, dewy grass beneath my broadening paws.

Cartilage pops, my teeth extend, and my snout lengthens until my female face is no longer identifiable. The unhinging of my jawbone turns a scream into an inhuman growl. Pain seizes me and I fear my heart is going to stop as the ungodly noise of my shift mingles with the sounds of those morphing around me.

Soon the pain fades, my body reforms, and I shake the buzz from my head as my wolf emerges. I sit back on my haunches and examine my paws, readjusting to the feel before I'm forced to perform for the master.

With the shifting complete, and given little time to adapt, a gunshot sounds and a hush falls over the courtyard. Head high I walk to the beginning of my course, Stone beside me facing his own obstacles.

I steal a sideways glance at him. He looks good. Strong. Well fed. Maybe he's the one 'doing it' with the master. Fit and muscular, he has at least a good forty pounds over me. His body is long where mine is short and his fur is dark where mine is light.

His big beefy paws sink into the grass, and he peels his lips back and bares sharp canines in an attempt to intimidate me. I ignore the grumble in my stomach and stare back. Tucking tail and fleeing is not an option.

A bird of prey squawks loudly overhead and flies toward the grapevines. I don't look up, it will only make me long for that kind of freedom, and right now I need all my wits about me.

A second gunshot cracks the air and as the smell of sulfur penetrates my senses, I dig my paws into the soft ground below and sprint forward, Stone easily keeping pace beside me.

Just then the clouds split open, the sun peeking out in time to catch the action. Panting beneath the glaring rays, my legs eat up the ground and I hit the first wall running. Concentrating on the rasp of my own breath and the pounding of my heart, I tune Stone out.

The silence of the crowd is broken by a chorus of frenzied barks at my rear. The sound of other wolves cheering us on makes me think of Jace and Clover and I push harder. They need me to win this. They need the nutrition I'll receive as a reward.

I scale the first wall. Easy. Then bolt toward the next obstacle, Jacob's ladder. With instincts guiding me, I begin my ascent, fully aware how the rungs get farther and farther apart.

I coach myself. *Easy, Pride. Slowly. Carefully. Don't look down.*

When I reach the top platform, I clamp the knotted rope with my sharp canines and bear down. My legs push off the ledge and I swing low, my paws mere inches from the ground as I cross the mud pit. An adjustment has been made and my light weight causes me to overshoot the sand by a few inches and I land with a thud onto the hard ground. I curse under my breath, determined not to make that mistake again. Blinking back the pain, I climb to my feet and shake it off. I don't bother to check on Stone. I can hear his pants and know he is closing the gap.

Up ahead is the net and I *know* what they've done, what Mario had been hinting at. This next obstacle could very well decide the outcome. Logic assures me that since Stone is big on strength and light on brains, he's bound to miss it.

I catch a flash of black fur as Stone runs by me. If he spots the flaw, I could end up going on scraps today. I can go on scraps. I've done it numerous times before. The aging Jace and Clover are another story and thoughts of them prompt me to dig in harder.

Stone bares sharp white teeth and glances at me over his shoulder as he takes to the outside edge of the net, where the netting hasn't been tampered with. Shocked, I open my mouth, but no sound comes.

He's already at the top of his net by the time I reach mine. He looks down at me and using telepathy, the way our kind communicates when in wolf form, barks out, *"What's the matter, Pride? Cat got your tongue?"*

I briefly note the way his aging bunkmates, Cruz and Star aren't cheering him on. Why would they? Greedy boy that

Stone is, he never shares his victor's reward with them. Not that we're allowed to share. But still, I don't let that stop me.

Getting my head back into the game, I scramble up quickly and drop to the ground on the other side of the net. Stone's inky black tail wags as he takes the lead. Determination renewed, I look at the strategically placed orange cones, not his tail.

He hasn't won yet.

I move in and out of the zig-zags, my small size and agility giving me an advantage over his larger, more muscled frame. I catch up with Stone and rage flashes in his pewter eyes as he angles his head to see me. That split second of inattention gives me the advantage. Wanting to drive home the fact that my brains have beaten his brawn, I grin and gesture toward the soft ground seconds before Stone's beefy paws sink into the trap, seconds before it's too late for him to do anything about it. When he stumbles, collective cheers ring out behind me. I jump over the man-made mud hole camouflaged by patches of green grass as the sound of Stone's teeth crashing together reverberates through the air.

I push forward, tackling the hurdles with ease and a few minutes later I reach the end. With a swish of my tail I turn to see Stone, now knee deep in mud. His nostrils flare, his teeth flash, and his eyes darken when he looks at me. In a swift movement that takes me by surprise, he leaps from the mud pit.

He exposes his fangs in challenge and instantly the air charges. Just like the animal he is, he turns on me. As I watch him, my mother's familiar warning words come rushing back.

*Trust no one but family.*

Despite our human halves, the wolves inside us are still primal beings, ruled by instincts and survival of the fittest. I can never let myself forget that.

I can feel the rage unfurling inside him as he lunges with

lightning speed. I go up on my haunches in response to his threat. He swipes at me, his long nails tearing past fur and catching the fleshy part of my cheek. I strike back, clamping my jaw around his jugular and dragging him to the ground. He proves too strong and within seconds he flips me over, promptly trapping me belly up between the ground and his powerful body. He flattens himself out along my length and puts his mouth near my ear.

"*I'm going to enjoy breaking you, kitty-cat,*" he murmurs.

I crinkle my nose, laugh and go straight for his ego. "*The only thing you can break is wind,*" I taunt in an attempt to rattle him.

Angered by my words he throws his head back and the deep sound coming from the depths of his throat sends a flock of birds into the blue sky. That gives me the opportunity to pull my legs out from beneath him and secure them under his stomach. With every ounce of strength I possess I push, sending him hurtling backwards. His howl stabs the air as he lands with a crash.

I climb to my feet and crouch low and note how much stronger Stone is getting. When he learns to fight with his head and not his heart, I'm going to be in big trouble. Right now he doesn't get it that there is no place for emotions in the battle of life and death.

Stone quickly rights himself and stalks toward me. As we square off again, guns cock above our heads and the master blows his canine whistle. Obedient dog that Stone is, he halts his forward momentum and shifts back to human. I watch him circle around and saunter off. I don't, however, miss the gleam in his eyes before he turns away—a gleam that speaks of secrets.

What does he know that I don't?

Crouched on all fours I quickly shift back to my human form and do something I haven't done in a long time. I touch

Stone's mind and the instant I do his dark, chaotic thoughts hit me like a sucker punch. My stomach twists in response and a hot wave of nausea rolls through me.

Determined to figure out what he knows before I break the connection, I push past the confusion. When I hear him erratically reciting a sequence of numbers I struggle to make sense of what he's doing. I go deeper and catch flashes of his cage, flashes of silver in a dark cellar. I hear footsteps followed by an ear-shattering gunshot. Then I see blood trickling between his lips, which not only alarms me but confuses me even more.

I press my hands over my ears to mute the thunderous sounds, and try to puzzle things out. None of it makes senses. If Stone had fought with a handler, I would have heard about it—news spreads quicker than a virus in the courtyard. But Stone would never fight with a handler. He's in tight with them and they give him way more leeway than the rest of us, which makes me wonder what's going on inside that head of his.

Then another more disturbing thought hits. Is this what happens to the mind once a wolf has been broken?

My chest tightens and I can't help but feel a pang of sympathy for him. Stone had been a good pup. A playmate.

A burst of sadness I can't allow myself to feel is quickly replaced by a cold shiver when Stone's hard eyes lock back on mine. He knows. He knows I've been inside. When I feel him searching, pushing his frenzied thoughts into my head, I go back on the defensive and immediately close off my mind.

Perplexed and feeling anxious after that brief encounter I summon my composure, climb to my feet and turn away in time to see the next two wolves line up for their test.

I move off to the side and spot Mario walking along the perimeter of the brick fence. He steps up to me, puts my collar back on and hands me my nightgown. A gunshot rings out as I pull it on over my mud-caked body.

"He wants to see you," he says and gestures with a nod. I don't need to look up to know who he is talking about. I can smell his expensive cologne and hear the squishing sound of his leather shoes on the ground as he approaches. I look up anyway.

My master...

The man who controls me.

I might be kept in the dark about most of the master's business dealings, but it's common knowledge among the wolves that he is deeply involved in the drug cartel. I smell it all over him. A tracker like me is called into action when something goes wrong. No one crosses my master and gets away with it. If you try, I'm brought in to make an example out of you, usually around the throat area.

I know what I'm doing is wrong. But I can't contain my wolf, can't fight the raging hunger gnawing at me. Maybe it would be different if I'd been taught. That's not part of my education though, because my master wants me to embrace my wild side. It does, however, give me some measure of comfort to know that the men I take down are no better than my master. Beneath their expensive cologne I can smell the greed, the deceit, the drugs.

"Good morning, Pride," the master says as he closes the distance between us. He smiles, but it doesn't reach his dark piercing eyes as they rake over me. The fine lines and creases on his face crisscross like a chain-link fence as he narrows his focus in concentration. Confidence oozes off his tall, powerful body, demanding the respect of those beneath his stature. Dark shiny hair frames a firm face, wrinkled and aged from too much time in the sun. With his dominant manner and well-groomed presence, if he were a wolf, he'd undoubtedly be the alpha. Today he looks relaxed and comfortable in his designer sports attire that, come afternoon, will be replaced by an expensive suit.

Strides determined, he comes closer and Mario steps away. My stomach growls and I wait for him to signal the handler to come back and take me to the kitchen. I won the race, which means I get to dine on the freshest food, not scraps or leftovers, and I always make sure to put some away for my bunkmates. At their age, even when pitted against their peers, they rarely win the race.

Still though, sometimes even when I perform my best I'm forced to go the rest of the day on very little. Even though I'm the runt, the master knows I come from good breeding and he has it in his head that I can always do better. Isn't beating a strong alpha like Stone in an extreme obstacle course enough?

He's not signaling a handler, which makes me think he has a job for me. He likes me hungry when I hunt. He thinks it gives me an edge.

"Master," I say.

He has that look in his eyes again. One that tells me a job needs to be done. He slips his finger under my chin, and I try not to flinch. I don't like to be touched, especially by him. My mother's touch was the only one I didn't shy away from. If I close my eyes real tight, I can almost remember what it feels like to be held in her strong arms, to be pulled into her embrace. I remember the way she had the uncanny ability to make me feel safe, even though I knew I was anything but.

The master's dark gaze moves over my face, assessing me, and I lower my eyes like any obedient canine would do. I might not be broken but I do know how to play the game. The stitched green alligator on his shoe, stark against the pristine white leather, glares at me, as if to warn: one wrong move and I'll eat you alive.

An odd, almost animalistic sound, rumbles in the master's

throat and my head jerks up with a start. I stare at his jugular as I sniff the air and can almost taste his excitement on the tip of my tongue. He always gets like this before a kill. Although gut instincts tell me there is something else going on inside his head. I can sense it. He wants something else from me.

But what?

"It's time, Pride."

My stomach clenches and my mind races. I really, really don't like the sound of this.

"Time for what?" I ask and stare him straight in the eyes, something us pups aren't allowed to do and I wonder if my disobedience will come with a price.

Instead of answering he gives me that confident smirk of his and says, "Get yourself something to eat, then get prettied up. I have a surprise for you."

**3**

*A surprise?*

The sick, uneasy feeling in my stomach tightens to a painful knot and a strange, horrible sense of foreboding crawls over my skin. I claw at my pale flesh, and despite the puffy, red welts rising up in response, I still can't shed the god-awful feeling that something very bad is about to go down.

As I consider this unexpected turn of events, the master snaps his fingers and gestures for Mario. A second later he pivots and steps away and I twist around to watch the handler's slow, careful approach. That's when my glance lands on Stone standing some twenty feet away. Looking hard and feral and dressed in nothing but a pair of worn jeans, I take note of the way he's watching me, the way he always watches me.

He has a smile on his face—smug, cocky and full of secrets—and it's all I can do not to cross the courtyard, extend my nails and swipe it off. My hackles bristle as I get the sneaking suspicion that Stone isn't quite as stupid as I always thought he was. When his cold eyes lock with mine it instantly provokes the wolf prowling restlessly inside me.

I stifle a growl, but the wide grin on his face, combined with the way his gaze has left mine to rake over my body, forces the sick feeling inside my stomach to punch into my throat. I swallow it down and try to figure out exactly what's going on.

Instinctively, fight or flight instincts kick in and my first reaction is to straighten my shoulders and assume a combative stance. Hardening myself, I offer Stone a look of cool indifference. The last thing I want is for him to sense my fear.

With my heart crashing against my chest, I take a step toward him, but when Stone manages to break through my mental shields, my legs stiffen beneath me and I gasp air.

He's in my head. I can feel him. He's doing something. But I can't tell what. I try to read him but his words are hurried, cryptic. As numbers ping around inside my brain, my throat tightens and I try to push him out. But he's too strong, too determined.

Before I can figure out what's going on, Mario steps up to me and his presence severs Stone's fierce hold over my thoughts. As I shoot the alpha a poisonous glare, hating his ability to fracture my barriers despite my resistance, he shoves his hands into his pockets and turns, leaving me standing there staring at his back as he saunters away.

As I watch him retreat my mind races, sorting through matters and doing a quick run through of the morning's events. I do a tally: the removal of my mother's empty cot, Stone's erratic behavior along with his talk of breaking me in, and the master's unexpected surprise.

My stomach churns faster as my thoughts come to a screeching halt. Flames race through my veins like aggravated fireflies, the flashes boiling my blood and fuelling the anger inside me. Feeling slightly off kilter, my legs wobble beneath me and I have to lock my knees to keep myself upright.

Oh God, he can't be.

But I'm a runt, I remind myself. *A runt!* No pack wants to breed any sort of genetic defect into the family. I suck in a sharp breath and as I consider that a moment longer my heart rate begins to slow. Okay, I have to be wrong. I just have to be because the alternative is too horrific to think about.

I spin back around to face my master, to demand answers, but only manage to catch a glimpse of his broad shoulders as he disappears into the house through his private entrance.

*What if I'm not wrong?*

The primal urge to shift, to run after him overcomes me. I toss my head from left to right, then block the blinding sun with my palm and focus in on all those beady little eyes glaring down at me from above. At that moment I don't care about the cocked guns or those six, trigger-happy fingers itching for me to make a wrong move. I gauge the time it will take me to reach my master's den, certain that I can make it there before the bullets engage and the gun powder explodes like the vineyard's deafening cannon.

Equal measures of fury and dread taunt my untamed wolf and there is nothing I can do to prevent those mixed emotions from slashing the barrier shielding my control. The second I give in to my animal impulses and unleash the wildness inside me, my nails begin to elongate and I can feel my wolf itching. She's waiting for me to give her the command to shift. Run.

Kill.

"Easy, Pride," Mario warns. He hooks a chain to my collar and gives it a good hard jerk, a reminder that shifting while leashed comes with a harsh price.

The cannon thunders in the distance at the exact same

moment the handler's words snap me back to reality, and my survival instincts kick in full force. I briefly pinch my eyes shut to help shake off the tantalizing call of the wild and search for a measure of control.

"Let's go," he says and I somehow manage to put one foot in front of the other while he leads me through the courtyard toward the kitchen entrance. With my head down I stare at the leafy blades of grass and the drying morning dew as we walk past the others. I ignore the two new competitors who cross in front of me. I don't want to see their faces. I don't want to meet their eyes. And I definitely don't want to know if they're aware of my fate, whatever that might be.

Once inside the estate a blast of cool air helps clear my rattled brain. I'm led through the kitchen to a windowless bathroom near the pantry. Mario waits outside and I close the door tightly behind me. As soon as I'm alone I let loose a long slow breath and wrap my fingers around the pedestal sink. I squeeze the cool porcelain until my knuckles turn white and my joints ache in protest.

I tip my head and spend a long time staring at my reflection in the vanity mirror, trying to figure out what it is about me that might have the master thinking I'm quality breeding stock. Not only am I too thin, my lips are too big, my cheekbones too high, and my dark eyes, which showcase unattractive smudges of sleeplessness beneath them, look so stark against my light hair.

I stand there well past my allotted time, and when I hear Mario growing restless in the hallway, I turn on the tap and splash my face with icy cold water. After washing up, I pull open the door and follow my handler back into the large, modern kitchen.

The scent of coffee teases my nostrils as we approach. We're not supposed to have caffeine but sometimes Mica slips me a small cup. I especially love the hazelnut-flavored beans, and could easily become addicted to the caramelized brew.

I drop down into one of the hard chairs, plant my elbows on the long oaken table and stare straight ahead at Mica. Dressed in a flared floral skirt and crisp white blouse tucked at the waist, she stands on the other side of the spacious room with her back to me as she fusses about with a loaf of stubborn bread. She gives the metal pan a good hard tap with her wooden spoon, and I watch Mario flinch as the sound echoes that of the starting gun outside.

A burst of warm air rushes inside when the side door opens and both Jace and Clover are led into the kitchen. Looking worn and tired they keep their heads down as Lawrence herds them back to the cellar.

Once they're out of sight, Mario steps up to Mica. They exchange a few words, keeping their voices low to prevent me from listening in with my exceptional hearing. A moment later Mica brings me a feast of fresh bread, butter, fruit, and bacon and eggs cooked the way I like them. Too bad I no longer have an appetite. Manners aside, I tear off a piece of warm bread and force myself to eat, because I somehow know that in the coming days, I'm going to need my strength.

Lacking her usual cheeriness, Mica moves about the kitchen and I don't question the peculiar way she's avoiding me. Clearly, she knows what my master's big surprise is and if it's upsetting her this much, then I know it can't be good for me.

*Could he really want to breed me?*

The bread in my mouth suddenly tastes like sawdust, and the small bite I'd managed to choke down only moments ago rises up for a second viewing and leaves a sour taste in my mouth.

"Pride?"

I lift my head at the sound of Mica's voice. "Yes?" I ask.

She looks at me long and hard. I can tell she wants to say something but when Mario clears his throat, like he's giving her some unspoken warning, she seems to change her mind and asks, "Would you like another slice?"

I follow her gaze to my palm and spot what used to be a slice of bread. Now it is nothing more than a ball of dough. Squished by my own hand.

I nod, then grab a napkin and fill it with fruit and bacon. Mica hands me two more slices of bread and as I add them to the pile I turn to Mario. "I'd like to go to my room now."

"My orders are to take you to Miss Kara."

I force a smile and show my compliance by saying, "I just need a minute to drop off my breakfast so I can eat it later." For good measure, I wipe the back of my palm over my forehead. "I think the heat is messing with my appetite."

He hesitates. He knows it's a lie because I'm *always* hungry. He also knows what I'm doing and even though sharing food is against the master's orders, he gives a curt nod and leads me downstairs. I'm suddenly grateful that it's Mario handling me today and not Lawrence. Lawrence would never have let me distribute one tiny crumb to my bunkmates.

Mario waits at the top of the landing and doesn't watch. I guess if he doesn't see what I'm doing he can't be held accountable for it. For a brief moment I feel sorry for him. After all, isn't he trapped here every bit as much as I am? At least he doesn't take pleasure in doling out abuse like Lawrence and a few of the other handlers do.

Moving quickly, I rush down the stairs. Both Jace and Clover rise from their cots when they see me.

"Pride," Clover rushes out, her eyes wide with apprehension. "What happened out there between you and Stone?"

I pass the napkin through the cage and as she gratefully accepts it, I briefly think about Stone's strange behavior. I don't want the elders to worry about me any more than they already do so I say, "It's nothing I can't handle."

Jace grasps the metal bars and squeezes until I see bone. Not that it would take much for the whites of his knuckles to show through his thinning skin, considering how underfed he is. There is a hitch in his voice when he says, "You need to stay away from him. He's up to something."

I look at Jace and could sob at the sadness I see on his face, the utter sense of helplessness in his milky white eyes when they meet mine.

A pang of sorrow cuts me deep at how broken the elders are, how defeated they feel. Unlike the other wolves, who mainly care about their own survival, Jace and Clover have shown me both empathy and compassion. I chalk it up to the forty or so years they'd spent living in the real world before their capture. My mother told me the two wolves took her under their care when she was first thrown in with them—perhaps because their own child had been killed in the cross-fire during their capture—and for that I'll always be grateful and indebted to them.

"I don't like the way he looks at you, Pride." The saggy skin under Jace's jowl tightens as he clenches down. "And he's growing strong. Too strong."

"I can handle him."

"I fear—" Jace begins, then stops himself.

"Fear what?"

"It's just..." his glance wanders to the empty cage and he doesn't need to finish his sentence for me to know what he's getting at.

Apprehension curls through me and my heart thuds against my chest. "I'll find a way to get us out of here before I allow that to happen."

Clover gives a worried shake of her head. "Pride—"

When Clover's words fall off, Jace reaches through the

cage and touches her shoulder. He gives a gentle, reassuring squeeze and the gesture is so warm and loving my throat tightens.

I tamp down those emotions and replace them with rage. Someday my master will pay for what he's done to us. "I'll find a way to get us out of here first. I promise."

Clover wrings her boney fingers. "You can't make that promise."

"I can and I will."

Worry washes over her once pretty face, now worn from years of abuse. "But your mother—"

When I hear a boot scuff on the stairs, I lean close and try to keep my voice from wavering. "My mother died trying to save me. Believe me, I hate that she died. I hate that they killed her, and while she couldn't give us freedom, she did give us knowledge. And knowledge is power, Clover. Her death won't be in vain. I can't let that happen."

"But the PTF..." she says, the fear in her voice reminding me we had more than our master to worry about.

As I think more about the PTF, I remember the one rule they are governed by: shoot first and ask questions later. Like other wolves, my mother used to be a productive member of society, secretly working side-by-side with humans, living a normal life in a small community and taking to the woods on shift night to avoid killing anyone. But to the PTF werewolves are still monsters that need to be killed.

My mother and her pack gained a lot of knowledge before their capture some twenty years ago, and from what she explained, the PTF are specially trained to spot a wolf in human form. They are educated at the best graduate schools, where they obtain master's degrees in sociology, studying everything from social relationships to species interactions and deviances. The officers are also trained by canine-behavior specialists. Detecting any wolf masquerading as a human is second nature to them.

"I'll cross that bridge when I get to it," I say, hoping I sound more confident than I feel.

The lines on Clover's face soften and I'm not sure if she's placating me or not when she says, "If anyone can do it Pride, it's you."

When Mario clears his throat, I step back. My chain clangs on the stairs as I take them two at a time to reach him. He doesn't speak. Instead he just grabs my leash and leads me to Miss Kara's suite on the second floor of the estate. Once there, he pushes open the double doors and the sharp tang of floral perfume assaults my sensitive nose.

Dressed in a fitted business suit, Miss Kara rises from her plush recliner, spreads her arms wide and starts toward me. "Pride, come in, come in."

I step inside and Mario moves in with me. He closes the door behind him and widens his stance to stand guard. Even though I've been in the suite hundreds of times, instincts dictate that I take a quick glance around and observe it anyway.

Warm rays of sunlight stream in through the large window and fall over the massive mahogany desk, and the piles of paper strewn across the top. A grooming station—or at least that's what I like to call it—complete with enough makeup and brushes to supply an entire town, fills the space on the opposite wall. A colonial door to my left leads into the bathroom. Miss Kara's suite looks more like an office/beauty salon than an estate bedroom. This is where she educates us, and teaches us all about manners and good grace. I often wonder if she came to this country to be a cosmetician. I'm sure, however, she wanted a better life than this.

She stands in front of me for a closer examination. Even without her two inch heels, Miss Kara is much taller than me, although I must say her lithe body seems equally as thin as mine. Unlike me, however, clothes don't seem to hang on her in the most unflattering ways. She dips her head and her big brown eyes scrutinize my curves, or lack thereof. Her nose crinkles in distaste and her painted lips pucker as she makes a tsking sound.

"We have so much work to do." She efficiently claps her hands, then points to the bathroom. "First let's get you showered. Now hurry."

I do as I'm told, but enjoy a few extra minutes beneath the hot steam, taking pleasure in the needle-like spray on my muddy body. I lather my hair with strawberry scented shampoo and scrub the obstacle course dirt from my skin with honeycomb soap that smells good enough to eat.

With my flesh practically rubbed raw, I climb from the shower, wrap a big fluffy towel around myself and exit the bathroom. Miss Kara guides me to the grooming station, running her fingers through my hair as we walk, and I take notice of the new white dress draped over her recliner.

The master often puts me in pretty clothes to lure my mark, especially when they're a difficult target. Perhaps there is nothing more to his surprise than that. A difficult mark in need of extra persuasion.

As Miss Kara seats me in front of the mirror, I try to engage her in conversation. With a nod, I gesture toward the dress and work to keep my voice light when I say, "It must be a challenging assignment if the master is putting me in something so pretty."

Dark lashes flash quickly over brown eyes and she keeps her expression blank when she answers. "It might be your most difficult assignment yet, Pride."

I don't miss the strange catch in her voice, or the flash of angst in her eyes before she quickly blinks it away. I get the distinct impression that she, too, is keeping something from me as I study her in the mirror and will her to look at me. But there is nothing I can do to make her meet my eyes.

Close to an hour later, after I've been plucked, perfumed and prettied up, Miss Kara splits the delicate dress down the back and I climb in from the neckline.

As it drapes my body I notice how easy it is to get in and out of. That detail might seem like a little thing to most but it's those little things that make a big difference on a mission, especially if I need to shift in a hurry.

I stare at my reflection and also notice how it accentuates what little curves I have and how the pretty diamond-like stones glisten in the overhead light. As I run my hands over the fake jewels I consider all the weapons I could make with them if only they were real.

When Miss Kara spins her finger, I twirl in front of the mirror and think the dress is beautiful. I keep that point to myself, but it doesn't stop me from longing to be a normal girl, one who might enjoy such nice things.

"You look gorgeous," she assures me, a look of satisfaction crossing her flawless, coffee-colored face.

A few minutes later she gives Mario a nod and the next thing I know I'm being led back downstairs and into the master's den.

Mario pushes open the door and ushers me inside. The second I step through the threshold and spot Stone sitting in one of the leather chairs facing the master's desk my stomach plummets.

My master waves a hand, an indication for me to sit in the empty chair next to Stone. At first I don't move, I don't think my legs will allow me to cross the room, but Mario nudges me from behind and it sets me into motion. I tug on my collar which suddenly seems to be cutting off my air supply and work to keep my emotions in check as I pad softly across the cool marble floor.

The master gives an appreciative nod. "You look very pretty today." When I don't answer, he hardens his voice and says, "Have a seat, Pride."

I lower myself. The whooshing sound the aged leather chair reminds me of flapping feathers and I can't help thinking how much I'd like to have my own set of wings right now so I could fly out the master's window and disappear into the wild forever.

Once I am seated, my master stands, walks to his mahogany bar and pours a generous amount of amber liquid into a small glass. I wish he'd get straight to the point, but instead he takes a hearty sip of alcohol, then pulls a gold lighter out of his suit pocket and lights a cigar. The pungent odor curls through the room, coats my throat like a thick layer of cotton, and threatens my gag reflexes. But I can't think about that right now. Not with the way the master has suddenly turned to me, his dark eyes more deadly than a silver bullet.

"Pride..." the master begins before taking a long hard pull of his cigar. I stare at him, and despite knowing better, I offer him my best cold face, but he doesn't flinch like the handlers do.

"Yes?" I ask.

A long pause and then, "I believe the time has come for you to take a mate."

"No!" I burst out and jump to my feet so quickly I nearly send the chair hurtling backwards.

My master looks past my shoulder and I barely hear Mario's quiet approach over the rapid pounding of my heart. I feel him move in close, ready to intervene should I get out of hand.

"It's time for you to breed, Pride." Everything in the way he's staring at me tells me it's not a suggestion, it's an order.

As my worst nightmare comes true, the entire room

begins to spin before my eyes and I lean forward to grip the edge of the master's desk to help stabilize myself.

"But I'm a runt," I say, then shoot Stone a pleading glance. "Why would you ever want to mate with a runt?"

Stone shakes his head in disbelief and the delight in his eyes as they trail longingly over my dress makes me shake with outrage.

"You have no idea, do you Pride?" he asks. "No idea at all."

No idea? What's he talking about?

"You *will* take him as a mate," my master insists.

"I won't," I shoot back, and the master gives me a warning glare, clearly angered by my defiance—a defiance that won't go unpunished, I'm sure. But why should I care about that? At this point any harsh punishment would pale in comparison to mating with Stone. "I'll fight him."

Ignoring my outburst the master says, "You will be placed in Stone's cell in six days."

Six days? Why six days? I struggle to think, then understanding hits.

*In six days the moon will be full. I will be at my most fertile and Stone will be at his strongest.*

"I won't do it," I say, and our eyes lock in a silent battle of wills.

The master drops his cigar into the ashtray and with two determined strides he crosses the room. He captures my face between his strong fingers and squeezes hard. From the corner of my eye I notice Stone toying with his collar and shifting in his seat. He has a strange expression on his face. It's one I've never seen before and can't quite identify.

The pain exploding in my jaw forces my focus onto my master. Even though his frame dwarfs mine, I jerk my head and stand my ground. His hold never wavers. His fingers bite into my flesh, but I know he'll never leave a mark on my cheek and risk disfiguring me. He needs my face unmarred and attractive if he wants me to lure his marks.

I continue to defy him by staring straight into his eyes. "Why?" I demand.

He laughs and eases off. "You're a smart girl. I thought you would have figured it out by now."

"Figured what out?"

"You're too wild, Pride, and don't for one minute think that I haven't noticed the way you're always listening and watching." He releases my face and steps back. "Motherhood is just the thing to tame you."

I give a very unladylike grunt and counter, "And you're going to risk breeding a genetic defect into the family so you can tame me?"

"Who knows, maybe we'll get lucky." He cocks his head and fixes me with a good hard look. "A pup will calm you down. If it doesn't then I'll be forced to kill you, like I killed your mother."

Rage surges up inside me and it takes every ounce of strength I possess to fight it down. If there is ever a time that I need to keep my wits about me, it's now. Instead of going for his throat and making him pay for what he did to my mother, I force myself to think with my head, not my heart. I avert my gaze and draw on my inner strength to help me shake off the anger.

Deep in my gut I know that someday, somehow his time will come, but with Mario standing so close behind me, a loaded gun in his holster, I know it isn't going to be today. I also know that getting myself killed isn't going to help me exact revenge, either.

With the distinct knowledge that my master is still holding all the cards, I take a calming breath and glance around. It's clear that I have to do something. It's also clear that I only have six days to figure out what it is I have to do.

"That's much better, Pride."

I lower my head and stare at the cold marble floor beneath me and decide, for the time being, that I'll let him think I'm playing it his way.

"Good girl," he says and twists on the balls of his feet to pick up his cigar. "I knew you'd come around." The master snaps his fingers and Mario steps away and opens the door for him.

"Stone," the master says as he tosses him a glance. "Since you were so efficient at disposing of the evidence after your last kill, I'll give you those five minutes alone with her, like you wanted."

The master grins at me. "I'm sure you have a lot to talk about before the big day."

After he leaves the room, Mario takes up his post by the door and keeps a watch over us. The sound of Stone climbing from his chair pulls my focus and I turn to him.

"I knew you'd look gorgeous in a dress." He gives me a wolfish smile as he stalks toward me.

I take a step back and snarl. "So you're the one who wanted me in this?"

"Yeah, I want you to wear it for our first mating." He darts a nervous glance toward Mario, then wets his lips as he focuses back in on me.

Once again I feel him surfing the outer barriers of my mind, trying to push his way in. To say I'm enraged is an understatement. I use every bit of strength I have to drive him back. I will not let him invade my privacy and the last things I want to hear are his erratic thoughts.

As rage mushrooms inside me, a smile softens his expression and he leans forward, like he wants to whisper something in my ear but I've heard all I've needed to hear so I press my hand against his chest to keep him at a distance.

"Didn't anyone ever tell you that it's bad luck to see the bride in her gown before the wedding?" I shoot back.

When Mario clears his throat, Stone's body stiffens and I can't help but think how odd he's acting. "Come on kitty-cat, it won't be so bad." He casually rolls one shoulder and laughs a little too loud. "Who knows, you might even like it."

At least he's right about one thing. It won't be so bad. Because as I watch his gaze move over my face, I make a silent vow to do whatever it takes to stop this mating from happening. Not only does the thought of him touching me make me sick, no way, no how am I about to bring puppies into this world to let them suffer at the hands of the master.

*ugust 24th, five days until full moon*

Silence hums overhead and practically deafens me as I jump from my cot and grip the cold, metal bars that keep me imprisoned. I cock my head and listen for sound, but the upstairs is quiet, no footsteps, no whispered words, and no rattling pipes, a good indication that the master and his staff have retired for the night.

Restless and edgy I twist my head and glance around my small cell. I fight down my feelings of anxiousness and suck in a breath but the air feels so heavy and suffocating I can barely inflate my lungs.

When my tired eyes fall on my ratty blanket, I smooth down my nightgown and stare at my bed with longing. While everything inside me urges me to rest—in the upcoming days I'll need to be fresh to win this battle—sleep continues to elude me. Every time I close my eyes I see Stone and that cocky smirk on his face, one that says he's finally going to defeat me.

Ice moves through my veins and I shiver, violently. Just thinking about Stone touching me, crawling over my body and claiming me as his mate has bile pushing into my throat. I try to swallow but my body is so dehydrated I'm unable to produce enough saliva to clear the bitter taste. I pinch my eyes shut and stifle a low, tortured growl. My hands squeeze the metal bar so hard the hinges begin to groan in protest.

When the sound curls under my skin, my eyes snap open and I instinctively test the durability of the cage. But if past experience has taught me anything it's that the bars are indestructible. Not even my wolf's strength can bend the reinforced metal. Instead of trying, I save my energy. As I work to calm myself I take in the empty cages beside me.

My gaze settles on the uneaten food that I'd distributed to my bunkmates earlier. From my short distance I can see the edges of the bread hardening, and catch the unpleasant tang of the warm fruit spoiling. I glance at the stairs then back to my victor's winnings, understanding someone pulled them out of here before they could eat.

Disturbed by that thought, I suck in another sharp breath, and that's when I get a whiff of the crispy bacon. The heady smell of meat might be tantalizing to my wolf, but under the circumstances my human stomach is too queasy to think about eating.

I'm sure news of my mating has spread through the pack and I can only hope that the master put Jace and Clover in another cell to prevent us from conspiring, from trying to find a way around his outrageous demands. But something in my gut warns that he might be using my empathy for my bunkmates against me.

Empathy is a weakness in this prison and although it's an emotion I've worked hard to keep hidden from my master, I realize he's cunning enough to understand I have concerns for the others, and he's cruel enough to use those concerns against me.

I can't bear to think about the elders, or what the master might have planned for them, so I turn from their empty cages and begin to pace, welcoming the feel of the cold cement pad beneath my feet. The damp floor feels icier than ever, and my pain censors react, sending warning signals to my brain. I should listen to those jangling alarms bells and climb into my bunk before I freeze the rough soles of my feet, but since I'm in need of a distraction, I embrace the pain and let it fuel my wolf. It's my pain that keeps my instincts sharp and helps me stay alive.

I continue to pace, and my thoughts bounce around my brain like a pinball as I work to strategize an escape. Even if I'm able to conquer the first roadblock and make it past the electric fence where would I go? How would I hide?

Would I head north, like my mother, and hope to find a pack that could help me? What if no such pack exists? What if it's only false hope?

I'm not sure where I'll go or what I'll do but decide to narrow my focus on the first roadblock at hand. As I wrack my brain, trying to figure a way around the fence, the hours slowly slip by, and soon enough I hear footsteps and muffled voices trickling down through the floorboards overheard. I still and stare at the door, waiting for what feels like forever for it to open.

Even more hours tick by and soon enough my bladder fills to the point of urgency, yet no one comes to my rescue. No handler has come to let the rebellious dog out. Then suddenly, understanding dawns in small increments. I'm paying for yesterday's disobedience.

Since I refuse to relieve myself in the corner, and give the master that kind of power, I drop to my knees and desperately try to ignore my body's basic needs. I spread out a thin layer of dirt and use it as a distraction. As I draw a picture of a beach, my own personal symbol of freedom, I repeat my mantra: I will not let him break me.

My senses perk when I finally hear the soft click of the lock overheard. I remain hunkered down in a defensive position and while I tune out the chaos erupting inside me, I mask my features and present a hardened exterior to my approaching handler.

Exercising caution, Lawrence descends the stairs slowly, but when a loud boom sounds from above, and the house practically rattles from the impact he braces himself on the steps. I wince at the sound, and choke back a cough as the noise disturbs a deep layer of dust on the overhead beams. My stomach drops and a terrible sense of foreboding fills me as small cloudy particles rain from the ceiling and wash out my drawing. I'm not superstitious, but I hate to think that it's a sign of sorts.

I wait for the aftershock. When none comes I can't help but think the commotion coming from above feels more like the wrath of the master and less like a California earthquake, which can't be good for any of us.

When the house stops vibrating, Lawrence resumes his approach, each menacing step meant to threaten my wolf and send it into hiding.

He exposes those rotten teeth of his and says, "Hey, kitten. The master wants to see you."

I glance up the steps and take in the slant of the sun on the barren stairwell wall. Judging by the angle, I can tell it's well into the late afternoon. As happy as I am to see daylight, I can't forget what the dawning of a new day really means. Five more sleeps until the full moon, until my fate is sealed.

Anger wells inside my gut but I push it down, knowing I

need to keep my head clear. I rise up from my crouched position and my lips peel back as I glare at Lawrence.

"What does he want?" I ask, even though I'm fully aware that Lawrence has no idea why I'm being summoned. When it comes to the master's business affairs, the handlers know little more than the wolves do. But I ask anyway because it's my way of reminding him that he's not all that high on the pecking order either.

"If I tell you, then I have to kill you," he taunts.

"Try," I say. I'm in such a foul mood that I don't even care what punishment comes with my disobedience.

His smile quickly dissolves and he throws my collar at me. With my lightning fast reflexes I catch it before it hits my face and that only seems to anger him more.

He exposes his gun. "Leash up, kitten."

As I snap my collar into place, my thoughts return to my master and I lose interest in sparring with Lawrence. Moving about numbly, I let Lawrence secure my chain and lead me toward the stairs. As I climb, I hear the other wolves in the courtyard. I listen for Jace and Clover, but can't quite distinguish their voices in the crowd.

A warm breeze carries the succulent scent of meat past my face, and my stomach rebels, a reminder that I haven't eaten since yesterday morning.

When we reach the landing, Lawrence guides me toward the hall but I stop outside the small bathroom door. He gives a ruthless yank on my chain and I grunt as it sends my body jerking forward.

I quickly regain my balance and our gazes clash in a silent battle. "Would you prefer I go on the master's floor?" I ask.

Something akin to fear passes over his eyes before he quickly masks it. Trying to look unfazed, he shifts on the balls of his feet, but I can tell he's uncomfortable and working hard to hide it.

"You have one minute."

He doesn't let go of my chain, instead he grips it tighter and stands guard outside the open bathroom door. I have to relieve myself so badly I don't complain. I dart inside, pull up my nightgown and quickly go about my business. Once complete I wash my hands, and then cup them to take a generous gulp of water. I glance in the mirror and see yesterday's makeup smudged beneath my tired eyes. It reminds me of how the master wanted me prettied up. Just thinking about him has the hairs on my nape prickling in warning.

What more could he want from me?

"Time's up." This time Lawrence yanks my chain so hard, it practically snaps my neck. A soft growl rumbles in my throat, and in an instinctive move my nails begin to elongate, my primal side wrestling for control.

He glares at me and moments before he gives the chain another savage yank—to keep the unruly pup in line—the master barks out an order from his office door. When the sound reaches our ears Lawrence straightens. Eyes wide, he pinches his lips together and they tremble slightly as they form a tight white line. He immediately falls into place in front of me and hurries down the hallway.

I follow Lawrence inside the office and instantly take note of the master's stiff posture as he speaks quietly into the phone. When he sees me, darkness clouds his eyes and he pitches his voice even lower, whispering in muffled words to prevent me from overhearing.

In an instinctive response my tongue darts out to taste the danger in the air. The unstable energy swirling around the room hits me like a slap to the face and triggers a reaction from deep within. As black angry waves roll off the master, my senses go on high alert, warning me. Every muscle in my body tightens, prepares. I'm not quite sure what's going on, all I know is that something very bad is going down. I can taste the tension and feel it in every fiber of my being. Then again, I'm not sure what could be worse than the news he delivered to me yesterday.

My gaze skates over the room and when no immediate danger presents itself to me, I let my glance shift to the bountiful spread of grapes, cheese, breads and those tiny finger sandwiches that I love so much. While it might simply be an afternoon snack for my master, there is enough food to feed me and the elders for at least a month. My stomach growls loudly, the noise filling the cracks in the walls as my hate for my master reaches new heights.

Lawrence looks on as hungrily as I do. When I hear his stomach's response I know it's his greed talking. He's already been fed today. The master diverts his attention and snaps his fingers at Lawrence. Lawrence's baggy jeans rub together and his heavy boots scuff the floor as he turns toward the door, to lock the others out, and us in. The bolt slides home and a moment later he drops my chain and nudges me forward.

Late afternoon sun trickles in through the open window and warms my bare feet as I shuffle along the polished floor. I stand there, and quickly catalogue the room a second time. That's when I notice the marble statue smashed on the floor, small broken pebbles are scattered around the master's desk. At least now I know what caused the commotion. But the sight of that broken statue alerts me to the master's rage and has me worried. The blood in my veins thickens and my pulse begins to jackhammer.

The master finally lowers the receiver and looks up from his desk. When I see darkness invading his cruel eyes, the inky black pupils bleeding into the brown, I instantly know why I've been summoned.

The lines beneath his eyes deepen as he gestures with a wave. "Have a seat, Pride." The master might be trying to present a calm demeanor, but I know it belies his true emotions. Anger resonates beneath each word, the cacophony of noise warning my wolf to tread carefully.

Once again my nape prickles and I draw on my inner strength as I stalk closer. I swallow and try not to stare at the scrumptious spread of food sprawled across my master's desk as I lower myself into the plush seat.

"Have you had anything to eat today?"

I steal a quick glance at him. His smile is brutal and twisted as he stares down at me, and while I know he's a hard man driven by greed my wolf still doesn't cower, like he wants her to. In fact, it's all I can do to keep her leashed and prevent her from going for his throat.

"Answer me," he demands, his voice lacking any sort of tolerance for me today.

I give a quick shake of my head.

"Then please, have a bite."

The nerves tracking along my spine tingle and I briefly meet his eyes, wondering what he's up to. I don't like it when he's nice to me. I know nothing good can come from it. As I consider his offer, the scent of the food calls out to me. I want to resist, I really do. I hate to take anything he offers me, but I'm so hungry I feel faint. If I try to escape when I'm this light headed, I wouldn't make it ten feet out the front gate.

After a quick consultation with myself, I slowly reach for a finger sandwich, then lean back in my seat to eat it.

"What have I done to deserve this?" I cautiously ask around a small bite.

The master props one elbow on his desk and scrubs his hand over his chin as he studies me. As I stare at him, I see an element of desperation on his face, one I've never ever seen before. It piques my interest and has my wolf stirring.

"It's not what you've done. It's what you're going to do."

Not at all surprised by that answer, I force myself to chew

slowly, even though I want to gobble it up and go for another. I continue to eat and try not to fidget, anxious to find out what's so important to the master that it's forced him to call on his best tracker.

Finally he says, "I have a job for you." When he leans forward and narrows those deadly eyes, I can smell something on him that I've never smelled before. Fear. It teases my wolf and triggers my senses.

As if to emphasize the importance of his next point, his voice takes on a hard edge when he adds, "And I need you to follow my orders exactly."

I swallow the rest of my tiny sandwich and gauge the master as I reach for another. He doesn't stop me and the fact that he's letting me have seconds can mean only one thing. He doesn't want my wolf ravenous during this hunt, doesn't want my carnal hunger getting the better of me. Whoever this mark is, he must be needed alive and that makes me curious. What threat does this mark pose to my master? How much would my master suffer if I purposely screwed this job up on him?

Then another thought strikes, and I nearly choke on my next bite.

The master is sending me out!

I can hardly believe it. After delivering yesterday's news, why would he take such a huge risk and allow me to leave the compound? I don't ask because I already know the answer. I'm the best tracker he has and this mark is important. But does he not understand that he'll be helping me past my first big roadblock, the electric fence?

Excitement wells inside me and I try to keep my face expressionless. I don't want the master to know what I'm thinking, but the telltale gleam in his eyes speaks volumes.

He knows I'm going to run.

The master gives me a small, shrewd smile that holds no

humor. "I'm sure you're smart enough not to try anything foolish."

Just then I hear voices in the courtyard. I glance out the window in time to see Mario lead Jace and Clover past the window. The bottom falls out of my world when understanding hits like a hard blow to the stomach. Air rushes from my lungs and my last vestige of control snaps like a taut wire.

"No!" I bark out, when I see the weariness on Clover's face. Her glance locks on mine and she mouths something to me. Something that sounds like *run.*

My heart seizes and I draw a savage breath. It's clear they know my fate—they also know theirs—yet they still want me to run, to fight back, to take over where my parents left off. They're willing to accept the punishment that comes with my disobedience.

Rage unfurls inside me and a growl rips from my lungs as I jump to my feet, but the gun cocking behind me is the only thing preventing me from shifting and crawling over the desk to tear flesh from bone.

Lawrence closes in from behind. "Easy, kitten."

My chest heaves as I glare at my master, my wolf scratching at my insides as she struggles to free herself.

He taps his fingers on his desk as we stare at each other, a silent battle of wills. A long moment passes before he asks, "Do we have an understanding, Pride?"

I don't answer. I can't. Instead, I continue to glare at him, chaos erupting inside me as the contents in my stomach churn and rise in my gut.

Believing he still has the upper hand, my master pulls a napkin off the table, shakes it out and lays it over his lap. He might as well be waving a red flag in front of a bull. My nostrils flare and I zero in on his throat.

Appearing unaffected by my outrage, the master doesn't

waste any more time with me. With a nod he gestures toward the door. "You leave at sunrise. Miss Kara will prepare you." And as simple as that, I'm dismissed.

Lawrence grabs my leash and yanks it, but I don't move. I can't tear my gaze away from the master's smug face, can't stop thinking about what he's going to look like when I'm through with him.

"Let's move." Lawrence's voice cuts through the riot pounding inside my head, and while I'm unable to settle my scattered thoughts Clover's last word keeps rushing to the forefront.

*Run!*

But how can I possibly run when he's holding all the cards?

How can I not?

I think of the puppies and the lifetime of abuse they're about to endure at the hands of the master. I think of the sacrifice the elders are willing to make, a sacrifice for me and a sacrifice for the greater good. In that instant I make a commitment to myself and vow their sacrifice will not go unavenged.

I'm going to crush him.

## 5

*ugust 25<sup>th</sup> Four days until full moon*

**T**he night is dark. The rain heavy.

From the back of the car I sink into the plush leather seat and listen to the mesmerizing drone of the wipers. They swish back and forth in a sleepy pattern as the driver negotiates the near deserted highway with practiced ease. The handler in the passenger seat leans forward and blasts the cool air to keep the windows from fogging and a bitter chill moves through me. Although I'm sure the chill has more to do with the deadly adventure I'm about to embark on and less to do with the frigid air nipping at my flesh.

On either side of me sit two body-guards, ones I've worked with before and know better than to cross. They're both big, brawny men with steroid-induced rage who wouldn't think twice of snapping my neck if I dared to even look at them the wrong way.

Following protocol, I keep my head down and stare at my hands, which are neatly folded and resting on my lap. I bide my time and try not to fidget under the uncomfortable tightness of my form-fitting jeans. While I'd like to adjust the waistband or at least open the button so I can breathe during this long car ride, I know better than to make any questionable movements. The results could be deadly.

I never travel with my collar on—how would that look if someone spotted it in passing, or if we were ever pulled over —so I currently have two cocked guns aimed my way with two trigger-happy men wielding them. They're cruel men, like my master, who love to torture and torment and I can tell they're just waiting for me to make one wrong move.

As I think about the risks I plan on taking a burst of anxiousness zings through my blood. I can't mess this up. I just can't. Too many people are counting on me and I refuse to let them down. Tonight is the night I have to escape.

Tonight is the night I *will* escape.

Then there will be no leashing my wolf, because no matter what it takes, or how long it takes, I'm going to put a stop to my master's cruelties once and for all.

I take a deep calming breath and pray the opportunity to get out from under the guards' watchful eyes presents itself. Otherwise... I quickly squash that thought. There cannot be an otherwise, because failure is not an option. I have to do this. For the elders, the puppies.

For my parents.

My chest squeezes as I angle my head and turn my attention back to the road. Earlier this morning, at the beginning of our long journey I'd paid extra attention to each twist and turn of the highway—I want to make sure I know my way back—but we've been driving for close to twelve hours and I've long ago lost track.

Once again I think of the elders and my stomach cramps.

I'll never forget that look on Clover's face, the one that reeked of resignation and utter loss. It's permanently etched in my memories and will always remind me of my mission.

Then I think of Stone, and what he wants from me. I can only guess the chaotic sequence of numbers running though his broken mind was some sort of countdown to our mating. As anxiousness mingles with rage, I use it, absorb it, and let it fuel the determination coursing through my veins.

A bump in the road and the flash of a highway sign have my thoughts careening back to the present. I'm able to read, *Olympic National Park, Port Angeles, Washington* through the blurry, rain soaked window before the plush SUV I'm traveling in speeds past.

I steal a glance around and try to gather my bearings. I've never been taken so far away from home before and I can't help but think how close we are to the Canadian border, to where those packs of wolves are rumored to run free. Wolves who hunt together and take care of each other. Wolves who haven't been confined and don't live by the same rules as we do—each wolf for himself.

Could such a place really exist? Do I dare hope?

Needing to occupy my thoughts to keep my emotions from getting the better of me, I consider the clothes Miss Kara dressed me in as I work to desensitize. My too tight-jeans feel like a second skin and could undoubtedly be considered provocative to some. The soft pink spaghetti-strap tank top clings to my body and douses my pale cheeks with a hint of color. Miss Kara fitted me with a lacy push up bra to give me a hint of cleavage, and while I don't think it suits me that well, it does make me feel feminine and maybe even a little pretty.

My long blonde curls are left loose and pinned in the front to better frame my face. My makeup is light and summer-time fresh, and the sticky gloss tinting my lips tastes like sweet watermelon. I can't seem to stop licking it. But I think the action has more to do with my nervousness and less to do with the sweet, fruity flavor.

My look is a youthful one, which leads me to believe the mark is close to my age. Of course, I won't be given his picture until moments before my hunt. I'm never told any more than I need to know, but *my* cover story, however, is usually the same. I'm new in town, a junior in high school, and I'm out looking to make a few friends before I begin classes.

We drive in strained silence, no music, no talking, only the hum of the wheels on the wet pavement and the drone of the wipers to cut through my thoughts. I should probably use this time to catch up on sleep, I barely captured a wink over the last two nights, but the closer we get to our destination, the more restless my wolf grows.

She can almost taste the freedom.

Not wanting to draw any unnecessary attention to my apprehensive state, I press shaky hands over my stomach and calm her. She settles slightly and hunches low, waiting.

Twenty minutes later we pull into a busy parking lot. The big SUV looks completely out of place as the driver squeezes it between two smaller vehicles. My muscles tense and I sit up straighter, scanning the area and taking in as much as I can.

From what I can tell we're sitting outside a motel in Port Angeles. At the far end, attached by a breezeway there is a restaurant or pub of some sort. Music pours from the open windows and above the long, aging building a neon sign advertising 'vacancy' is flashing in an erratic pattern.

Moments before the driver turns the car off, the handler to my right cracks his window. I instantly notice the dip in temperature. Wherever we are we must be at a higher elevation. At home in the valley the air is warm and sultry, even this late at night. Here in this mountain town, with the huge, snow-capped peaks providing a gorgeous backdrop to the motel, there is a bite in the air, one I've never quite felt before. My wolf bristles, anxious to climb those hills and feel that cool wind whipping across her face.

The driver shifts in his seat and hands me a file. Since he knows how well I can see in the dark he doesn't bother to flick a light on. I lay the file on my lap and carefully peel it open. The first thing I notice is the swatch of material provided, the second thing is the mark. My wolf gives a little yelp, but I try not to show any sort of emotion as I stare at the photo. It becomes painfully apparent why they needed a young, fresh-faced girl for this job—or at least a wolf who can pass herself off as one. My mark is just a boy, merely a couple years older than me.

My heart sinks a little and my stomach turns inside out as I commit his features to memory. He doesn't look like any drug lord I've ever tracked before. I take a good long sniff of the swatch and place it back in the file before I close it. Taking extra care to harden my features, I hand it back.

The truth is, it makes me sick to my stomach to think the master is hunting someone so young. I can't imagine what he might want with him, or worse, what he might do to him. But I do console myself with the knowledge that the boy will have a fighting chance to flee, because this time, I have no intention of following the master's orders.

Just thinking about running has a fresh wave of anxiety rushing over me. My fingers instinctively go to my neck, and I feel the microchip planted below my skin.

Despite the cool temperature outside, sweat beads on my forehead and I inconspicuously wipe my brow. I know I have to maintain protocol and keep suspicion off me until I can break free, so I take a moment to go over the instructions that were carefully drilled into me this morning. Using feminine appeal—not that I think I have a whole lot of that—I'm to flirt with the mark and lure him to the car, where I'm to then hand him off to the bodyguards. I'm only to call on my wolf if he gets suspicious and tries to run.

Then the rules change.

I'm an excellent tracker, and it won't take my wolf long to find him. Once captured, I'm to lead him back. If he resists, I attack. Not to kill him, just enough to scare him and draw him out of the woods. Once my wolf gets the taste of blood, however, it can be hard to marshal her, especially when she's hungry. I guess that's why the master fed me so well this morning.

I wipe my palms on my jeans before the bodyguard opens the door to let me out. I cringe against the overhead light as he glances around to make sure the coast is clear. Once he's satisfied, he climbs out and gestures for me to follow. I slide across the leather and inhale the night air as I firmly plant my feet on the wet pavement. Hard rain slaps my cool skin and a big fat drop lands on my tongue as I glance skyward.

I'm grateful that it's raining because it's always harder for the handlers to track us wolves in wet weather. If the rain slows them down enough perhaps I can lose them by running long and hard and putting a great deal of distance between us. Or perhaps the heavy rain will cause static and interfere with the microchip's radio frequency. Hope fills me, but I keep it from my face.

From the front seat, the handler shoves a raincoat into my hands. "Keep yourself presentable," he says.

I shuffle into the coat and pull the hood up to keep my hair dry and my makeup from spilling down my face. A quick nod to my bodyguard lets him know I'm ready.

I step ahead, shift into character by pretending to be an innocent seventeen-year-old girl, and make my way to the front entrance. The bodyguard remains a few feet back and we pretend we don't know each other.

As I approach the wooden door, my glance keeps wandering to the distant mountains scattered through the Olympic National Park. My wolf stirs, wanting that kind of freedom. In search of an escape, I scent the air and can almost smell the earthy ground and fresh pine trees. My ears perk and catch the sound of the water rushing down the rocky embankments. As the wild calls out to me, my wolf grows increasingly restless, itching to run up that cliff, and lose herself in the night.

*Shhh,* I whisper under my breath in an attempt to settle her.

When my hand closes around the door knob, I tune the world out and focus on one thing and one thing only. Escape. I blink the water from my eyes as I step inside and pull down my damp hood.

A quick casual glance around lets me know the place is busy. I suppose that's to be expected on a Saturday night, but it does make zeroing in on my mark a bit more difficult. Not that I'm going to hunt him, but I can't deny that my curiosity is piqued. That, and I have to let my handlers believe I'm doing my job. Anything out of the ordinary will simply raise suspicion.

I think more about my mark. From his picture alone I can tell he's no drug lord. So who exactly is he and why is he so meaningful to my master?

I shrug out of my jacket, step farther into the establishment, and catalogue my surroundings. Using caution, I look for possible threats and deadly enemies, as well as my best escape route.

Beneath a row of small windows a string of padded booths are neatly aligned along the wall. I spot a few couples talking quietly over drinks, their hands touching shyly, and the normalcy of it all makes my gut clench.

Squared wooden tables, scratched and dented from years of misuse, are haphazardly scattered throughout the floor and seem to be occupied by those who haven't hooked up yet. I take note of my exits. Other than the door I came in I can see another door toward the back. A service entrance. Perfect.

The crowd is young like me. But unlike me they're loud, rambunctious, and despite their barely-legal drinking age, a vast amount of alcohol is being consumed. A plume of cigarette smoke curls in front of me and the pungent scent mingles with a mixed bouquet of perfumes and assaults my sensitive nostrils.

I crinkle my nose as I cut through the throngs of people and the sound of balls breaking, followed by a woman's laughter, filters in from the back room. I shoot a glance to my left and wonder if there is an exit back there as well.

With my bodyguard at my back, I make my way to the bar. When I take a seat on the hard wooden stool, I scan the area behind the counter and take note of the glass shelves filled with liquor bottles and the floor-to-ceiling mirror that allows me to see behind my back without having to turn. The elderly gentleman working the counter moves in front of me, blocking my view of the mirror. He eyes me skeptically and I wonder if he's about to card me.

"I'll have a coke," I say before he gets a chance, then I shoot an innocent look over my shoulder. "My mom's checking in. I'm waiting for her."

As I sit there blinking up at him, he nods and pours me a soda before moving on to the next client. I take a small sip of my drink and spin on my stool.

That's when my glance lands on him.

At first sight air hisses from my lungs and I don't need to

weed through the smells clouding the air to know it's the boy I was sent to hunt.

My hackles twitch as I watch the way he turns toward me. He shifts in his seat, each movement careful, purposeful.

Dangerous.

There is an intensity about him that I've never seen before, one that has my wolf stirring in the most bizarre ways.

From across the room our gazes collide and lock and, oddly enough, as we continue to stare at one another I feel a little disoriented, a little thrown off my game. The rest of the crowd seems to fade away and when my pulse kicks up a notch and pounds at the base of my throat I get the feeling there is more to this boy than meets the eye.

Carrying himself like a skilled predator, he has his back to the wall, keeping one eye on me and the other on the door. He looks at me long and hard, and his gaze is so unwavering and so penetrating that it practically robs me of my next breath.

Feeling a little peculiar inside, my glance trails over him, and I can't help but notice how strikingly handsome he is. Dressed in a navy t-shirt and a pair of faded jeans it should be easy for him to blend and lose himself into the crowd. But he doesn't. At least not to me.

When my body reacts strangely, I give a quick shake of my head to clear it, hardly able to believe my reaction to this boy.

This mark.

My gaze travels back to his face and haunted eyes with a lifetime of secrets lock back on mine. Foreign sensations erupt in my stomach when he blinks dark lashes over liquid blue eyes. I swallow. Hard. Because there is something about those vibrant blue eyes of his that remind me of the Pacific Ocean—remind me of freedom.

I sit there and try to still my heart, and despite everything warning me to, I can't seem to pull my glance away, can't seem to turn from him. What is it about this boy that holds my attention and fills me with curiosity, fear?

I take a moment and wonder what he sees when he looks at me. Does he see a young runt, eyes too big, lips too full and skin too pale? Or does he see a girl? One, who, under different circumstances he might approach and ask to buy a soda. One he'd consider bringing home to meet his parents.

My heart beats faster and I can feel my chest rising and falling as I get lost in that girlish thought. For a moment I forget who I really am. For a moment I allow myself to dream. But when reality comes creeping back, like it always does. I fist my hands until my nails penetrate flesh. I'm not a normal girl and I can never have a normal life.

*Get your head back in the game, Pride.*

Rattled, I work to harden myself, to focus, but when his lips turn up at the corner, the hairs on my nape tingle, like they always do when my wolf senses danger. Then it suddenly occurs to me—he knows. *He knows what I am!* And he knows why I'm here. My blood rushes and my animal instincts go on high alert.

I narrow my eyes suspiciously and study him harder. He, in turn, lazily drums his fingers on the scarred tabletop and inspects me. His glance is tentative, searching, deeply probing and I don't miss the curious lift of his dark brow as we size one another up.

For some reason I get the distinct impression that not only does he know what I am, but that he's been waiting for me. My ears perk as I listen to the blood in his veins. It's slow and steady, a telltale sign that he's not afraid, at least not of me.

With confidence oozing off him in waves, he continues to drum his fingers and I shift on my stool, uncomfortable under his careful scrutiny and concentrate on the one question that keeps circling around inside my head.

Who is this boy?

I take in his face, his brown, shoulder-length hair, the pretty flecks of pewter in his blue eyes—tiny flecks of pewter that weren't there a moment ago.

Oh no!

My body tenses and it takes every ounce of strength I have to keep from flying out of my chair, shifting mid-air, and pouncing on the boy who is studying me with intimate recognition. Because this boy isn't a boy at all.

He's a wolf.

*A shifter, like me!*

But he's not just any shifter. He's an alpha. One who is dark and dangerous and could tear my head clear off my shoulders before I could even think about bolting.

My heart drums in my ears and as I tear my gaze away my survival instincts kick into high gear. I need to move. I need to run. I need to do something.

My glance flutters around the room to catch sight of my bodyguard. He's watching me, but he's also watching the cute brunette two tables over. My pulse pounds so hard in my neck I fear some vital organ in my body might explode. But I can't think about that right now. Because right now, with my guard's attention diverted, this might be my only opportunity to run. I wet my dry lips and swivel on my chair, calculating how long it will take for me to reach the back exit. I'm fast, but my mark looks faster.

Moments before I'm ready to bolt I steal one last look at the boy, but when I notice something on his neck it stills me and has warning bells clanging in my head.

I look closer, to make sure, but there is no denying what I see. The boy has chafe marks on his neck.

Chafe marks where a collar used to be!

As the room spins before me, my hackles bristle, and I falter on my stool. When my feet hit the floor, my shaky legs almost give out beneath me because it suddenly becomes glaringly obvious that boy is not just a shifter.

He's a tracker!

As my brain works through various scenarios, my throat closes over. Is it possible that *I'm* the mark? That the master has finally grown tired of my disobedience and has driven me out here to a place where I can never be traced back to him, to dispose of me swiftly and cleanly.

Desperate to understand who this tracker is, where he's come from and what he wants I try to read his thoughts, to see if I can speak to him telepathically in human form. As I struggle to communicate, my gaze focuses back in on his neck, and that's when I see the tiny scar below his jugular.

Taken aback by that discovery, my blood rushes faster and a million questions race through my mind. Mainly, how did he remove his microchip? And how did the handlers find him without it?

Before I can seek answers to those questions the heavy front door pounds open and a hush seems to fall over the crowd. I turn and bite down a strangled cry when my glance lands on two officers, but I instantly know they're not any old run-of-the-mill officers. From the way they are sniffing the air and carefully scanning the establishment, my gut warns that I've come face to face with members of the Paranormal Task Force.

And they're on the hunt.

I slide back on my stool and turn from them to face the bar. My stomach plummets when I catch my reflection in the mirror. I can see undisguised shock and fear spreading across my face. I try to wipe it off, try to pull off casual, and try to act like I'm nothing more than a normal girl out looking to hook up with a normal boy.

From my peripheral vision I spot the alpha. He looks worried, afraid, and just as surprised by this turn of events as I am. His blood rushes faster and his hands are fisted so hard I can see the whitening of his knuckles. His fear fuels my wolf and I can feel her stirring, itching to come out of hiding. But I must keep her leashed. If I don't I'll never make it out of here alive.

*Breathe, Pride, breathe.*

But I don't breathe, instead my blood runs cold and I make the mistake of catching the PTF officer's eye in the mirror. The look on his face is beyond frightening, and I instantly know when my act failed, when those deadly men who've been trained to shoot first and ask questions later have made me for what I really am. A wolf in girls' clothes.

As ruthless eyes lock on mine, the officer's hand hovers over his gun, his fingers twitching. In an instinctive reaction my lips peel back to expose sharp teeth, and my snout begins to elongate.

I spot another officer closing in from my right and I quickly calculate my odds. My wolf, as fearless as she might be knows there are too many of them to take on alone. Fight-or-flight instincts kick in and dictate I run. My heart races faster and as I prepare to make my move a hand slams down on my shoulder.

Frantic, I open my mouth but the look on the boy's face when my anxious glance searches him out silences me. In the face of a common enemy we connect on an instinctive level, and understanding arcs between us. Our eyes lock and we communicate silently, with only one thought propelling us both on—survival.

The boy begins to move so fast I can barely keep track of his whereabouts. The next thing I know the mirror behind the bartender shatters and liquor bottles smash to the floor.

Shrill screams sting my ears as flames ignite and lick up the walls in a mad rush.

A commotion breaks out around me, and I use that distraction to break free from the officer's firm hold. Dashing around the flurry of people, I dart to the back of the pub, to where the boy stands waiting. The alpha might be dangerous, but I'm smart enough to understand that right now, as I face death at the hands of the PTF, this deadly shifter is the lesser of two evils. Better the devil you know, as my father used to say. Not that I know this alpha, I don't. But I do understand canine behavior.

"This way." Moving with confidence, he kicks open the service door and ushers me outside.

My heart is beating so fast I can barely breathe, let alone think. I let my wolf instincts take over and follow the alpha into the dark, wet night. Once outside a rush of cold air slaps my face, and I turn to watch him secure the door behind us.

He grabs my hand and his voice is deceptively calm when he says, "Come on. We don't have a lot of time."

Smoke rises from the building and hangs over the forest like a deadly noose as we rush toward the trees at the far end of the lot, to where the rain doesn't reach us. Cloaked in darkness, we duck low and try to camouflage ourselves beneath the tall timber.

The sound of someone kicking the door startles me and I glance over my shoulder. Gnarled roots twist beneath my sandals and I cringe as the sound saws through the night. Hinges groan and within seconds the service door breaks open. Shards of tiny wooden splinters shower through the air and a moment later I blink against the flashlights aimed my way.

We jump to our feet, run deeper into the woods and hide behind a towering tree. I press my back against the thick trunk and the scratchy bark scores my skin as I peer into the ominous night. Breath ragged, my glance rips from left to right as I work to devise my next move.

Before I can come up with anything concrete, the boy tears his shirt from his chest and I catch the scent of his clean, soapy skin as he undresses. Unable to help myself, my glance races over his body—one that lacks my scars.

I try to keep my voice level. "What are you doing?"

"We need to get out of here," he barks out, snapping my attention back to his face.

*We?*

Exercising caution I begin to inch away, sliding along the massive tree and putting some well-needed distance between us. My escape plans do not involve running with a dangerous alpha wolf, one who is wanted by my master. This boy is simply another obstacle I don't need.

Once again my gaze goes to the collar marks and the tiny purple scar near his jugular. He might be a shifter, a powerful one at that, and while he helped me escape, he's still a stranger to me. One I don't trust.

"I run alone."

In a move so fast it takes me off guard, he pulls a knife and presses the cold steel blade to my neck. His intense, penetrating gaze moves over my face and when he opens his mouth I can tell he's trying to choose his next words very carefully.

Since his actions prove threatening, my wolf stands at attention, awaiting my command. The shifter looming over me might be big and deadly, but my primal side isn't about to back down. I'm smart enough, however, to keep her leashed for the time being. At least until I hear what he has to say.

The sharp blade splits my flesh and the coppery scent of blood reaches my nostrils. Our glances collide and a dark shiver trickles along my spine. As the air charges, I hold off my wolf and stand my ground.

The pewter in his eyes deepens when he pushes the knife in harder. "You won't make it very far with this."

I know what he means. What he wants to do. But what if it's a trick? What if he's one of my master's puppets, sent to cut my jugular and leave me for dead?

What if he's not?

**6**

As indecision flickers through me, I quickly weigh the risks. In that instant I realize I have little choice. My best chance of losing those hunters and making out of this place alive is to let this boy slice into my neck.

I grip his hand and press the steel blade of the knife harder into my throat. "Do it."

My wolf bristles. She doesn't like it, but that doesn't stop me from placing my fate in this stranger's hands. I don't do it because I believe in him. I don't. I do it because the next few minutes are about survival, not trust.

His face hardens and the pewter flecks recede as his wolf settles. Big black irises swim in a stormy sea of ocean blue as he tips my chin up and searches my throat. I don't like to be touched so I try not to flinch as his deft hands surf over my throat, inspecting and probing until he finds exactly what he's looking for.

"Don't move," he warns in a hushed tone. His voice is both hard and fierce and has my composure slipping a little.

But I've made my decision and I refuse to second guess it now.

As tightness settles in my chest I tune out the footsteps pounding toward us and focus on the fierce concentration moving over his face. It's that fierce concentration that gives me hope that this rogue tracker knows what he's doing.

With a sweep of his hand he pushes my hair off my shoulders, and something in the careful, delicate way he touches my skin sends shockwaves rocketing through my body. A shiver rushes over my flesh and there is nothing I can do to stop my body from trembling.

His eyes meet mine for a brief second, and when he searches my face I almost forget how to breathe. "Easy there, little one," he says. His breath rushes over my cheeks and the softness I hear in his cadence almost chases away my anxiousness. Feeling a little rattled by my responses to him, I force my stiff muscles to relax and take deep centering breaths, in through my nose and out through my mouth.

With the PTF hot on our tails, not to mention my handlers, the forest around us begins to shake from the thundering chaos. As the hunters fan out in different directions, the ground vibrates and the wind picks up, blowing damp leaves and debris past our faces. Trees quake in response, sending the nightlife into hiding.

The rain falls harder and penetrates the canopy of branches overhead, soaking my clothes and hair and making the dangerous removal of my microchip that much more difficult. As my drenched top clings to my body a savage chill settles in my bones. Goosebumps break out on my flesh and I try not to shiver as I allow this boy to split my skin.

Despite the urgency of the situation he doesn't hurry. Slow, steady hands move over my neck and not only am I surprised by his dexterity, I'm surprised by his gentle touch, especially since all I've ever known is brutality from men.

I feel a sharp sting, and then his glance meets mine as his hand hovers over my neck. Skilful fingers remain motionless in mid air, waiting for me to react. I hold still as a fierce wave of light-headedness washes over me in a debilitating whoosh. But I don't let it weaken me. Instead I bite back an animal cry and let the pain strengthen my wolf.

"Brave little girl," he whispers, and I want to correct him. I might be brave, and I might be a runt, but I'm no little girl. Like him, I'm a tracker, and while I might not be an alpha, when it comes right down to it my wolf will do whatever it takes to survive.

He turns his attention back to my throat. Squeezing my skin he pushes his knife in deeper to catch the underbelly of the device. A quick flick later, he holds a blood coated, circular piece of plastic between his fingers.

After he shows me the microchip, he says, "Let your handlers track this." Turning from me, he tosses it far into the woods.

My ears perk, listening for it to land, but my attention is no longer on the tracking device, it's on the river of blood trickling down my neck. Within seconds my tank top turns a deeper shake of pink, the coppery scent rising like cool mist on a placid lake until it reaches our nostrils.

As the alpha's glance carefully tracks the rivulets of crimson trickling along my throat I don't miss his deep, agonized growl as it rumbles in the night.

Looking fierce and carnal, he licks a fat water droplet from his mouth and that's when I see the bloodlust flashing in his eyes. My senses go on high alert and everything inside me warns that this boy, this big bad wolf, would like nothing better than to eat me alive.

His hand jerks out. I instinctively take on a combative stance but he simply reaches behind me to grab a few leaves off a bush. He shoves them into his mouth, chews, and then places them on my cut. My cold skin begins to tingle as the plant goes to work on nursing my sore.

I eye him carefully. "What's that for?"

"Infection."

Puzzled, I glare at him. We both know as soon as I shift into wolf form, my body will heal itself. In a few days all that will be left is a purple scar. I'm about to ask what's really going on, but he steps closer, too close. His big hands span my waist and when I try to move away he anchors me in place.

He puts his mouth close to my ear and his voice is low, so low it takes effort for me to hear him. "The name is Logan."

Sensations begin to swell inside me, confusing me to the point of distraction. Since I need all my wits about me, I quickly try to tamp them down.

"Pride. It's Pride," I rush out in a tight whisper before I can think better of it.

I instantly want to take my words back. I know I shouldn't tell him anything about me let alone give him my name, but there is something about this boy that's throwing me off balance.

I've never reacted to another wolf this way before and not only do I despise what he does to me, I can't seem to make sense of it.

Then again perhaps it's simply animal instincts. A female is programmed to seek a dominant male. In the wild, survival of the species depends on it.

Either way there is one thing I do know. He's a distraction I don't need, a ruthless one at that, and the sooner I get away from him the better.

His deft fingers begin to loosen my shirt. As he tugs my tank top out of my waistband, helping me from my clothes, the soft pad of his thumb brushes over my sensitive flesh.

*What does he think he's doing?*

My predatory instincts take over and I react to his unwelcome touch. Angered and unafraid, my wolf growls a warning and my canines sharpen, putting a stop to any further intimate exploration.

He inches back, and I instantly understand his intent as his hands go to his buckle. He unfastens his pants and with a nod he gestures toward a distance peak. "We need to get into a defensive position."

I almost feel foolish that I'd mistaken his gesture for anything more than what it was. I'm a runt, nothing more, and undoubtedly considered one of nature's mistakes to an alpha like him. But he doesn't give me time to dwell on the illogical notion that he was undressing me for other purposes. With hurried movements he begins to shed the rest of his clothes and instead of following suit, I simply stand there and watch.

His voice takes on a hard edge, one that warns me not to challenge this alpha when he says, "We need to go. Now."

I glare at him and want to remind him that I travel alone. But when voices thunder nearby, the hunters growing dangerously close, I realize I'm in no position to argue. He's right. I need to move. Now. I reach for the hem of my tank top.

Like any good tracker, Logan makes quick work of his clothes, discarding them in record time. Normally I don't watch when another shifter sheds, but there is something about this boy that holds my attention.

Without a hint of modesty, he finishes stripping, then stands before me completely naked. As I take in his body my wolf reacts. My blood pumps faster and a strange, primal growl rips from my throat before I can stop it.

I've seen naked before, but I've never seen this kind of naked. A wave of awareness moves through me and throws me off balance. I shake it off, hating the primal effect he seems to have over my wolf.

My glance travels back to his face and I catch the way he's staring at me. His body is tense and with the hunters closing in he presses a finger to his lips and silently communicates with his eyes. We exchange a long glance and I know what he wants, what he's waiting for.

My hands grip the hem of my tank top tighter and for the first time in my life I feel self-conscious about getting naked in front of a boy.

I brush that ridiculous emotion aside and remind myself that at our core we're animals, ruled by nature and survival of the fittest. Shedding in front of another shifter is as natural as breathing.

I pull my top off and hurry out of my bra and jeans. When I hear Logan take in a sharp breath, my glance darts to his and my muscles tense in response to his expression.

A deadly mixture of surprise and anger registers on his face, and the pain in his gaze has me leaning forward to let a long curtain of blond hair cover my bare, damaged flesh—for both our sakes.

His eyes search mine, and while he's a dangerous alpha something in his soft whisper reminds me that he's still just a boy, "I'm sorry, Pride. My master wasn't so cruel."

Before I can tell him that I don't want his pity, he turns from me, and I get the impression that he's offering me his back not because he can't stand to see my scars, but because he's gifting me with a measure of privacy.

Shocked, I don't know what to make of it—or him. No one has ever treated me like a human girl before, but I have no time to think about it. I hear twigs crunch and quickly scent the air, only to discover that a hunter is merely a few feet away from discovering us.

Logan drops to the ground and I quickly peel off the rest of my clothes and let my animal instincts take over. When I finish transforming, I seek him out. Looking fierce and deadly, he's already on all fours, waiting for me, his pewter eyes glistening like precious gemstones in the dark.

*"Ready?"* he asks.

Since he seems to know more about where we need to go than I do, I make the quick decision to follow him, for the time being. Then I'll make a clean break after the PTF and handlers lose our trail. I nod my head and lope toward him.

*"Stay close."*

With a flick of his tail, he takes off ahead of me, and as I follow behind I can't help but think he is the most powerful wolf I've ever seen. Long lean legs flex as he runs, jumping branches and negotiating the dark forest with practiced ease. Wind rushes through the trees and washes over his streamlined frame, matting his thick brownish-black fur to his body.

We run long, hard and well into the night and his speed, strength and stamina impresses me as we cut across the rough terrain. I continue to keep pace as the moon rises higher and higher in the sky. Soon I find myself so deep in unknown territory that I fear it could take me days to scent my way out. The air grows colder and grass turns to snow as we continue our ascent up the side of a mountain. I paw at the white flakes, and marvel at the way they feel beneath my rough pads.

After running for what could very well be hours, Logan slows to a trot, and I canter up beside him, keeping a cautious distance. That's when I notice how high up we are. Ice crunches beneath my paws as I move to the cliff's edge and look out over the terrain below. I gasp, never having seen anything quite so incredible.

But I shake my head, unable to think about that. Instead, I memorize the landscape and work to pinpoint my coordinates. I recall the large post boards we passed during our climb, advertising the different hiking trails throughout the park, not to mention the warning signs, indicating the dangerous animals that inhabit the sanctuary. I've never heard of the Olympic National Park before, but from my elevation I can see for miles, and what I see fascinates my wolf. She wants to stay. She wants to call this home.

"*Nice, isn't it?*" The sound of Logan's voice inside my head startles me, and reminds me that I'm not here to enjoy the view.

"*Hey...*" he says, coaxing me when I don't answer.

He stalks closer, close enough for our breaths to mingle. As his scent fills my nostrils I can tell he's trying to lighten my mood and lift my concerns, but he has no idea how deep my worries run. Escape from the compound might be the end for him, but this is the beginning for me. I have a greater purpose.

With a playful flick, Logan nudges my chin with his muzzle. I turn from him and his voice is full of youthful excitement when he says, "*What's the matter Pride, cat got your tongue?*"

A growl rips from my throat and I turn on him. "*Don't say that to me.*"

Our gazes clash and he lifts a paw, reacting like he'd been struck. "*Hey, I didn't mean...*"

I step away and consider the night's events as I walk along the jagged edge. In the face of a common enemy Logan and I might have connected, but that doesn't mean I trust him, or want to crack jokes with him as we admire the scenery.

In our world it's every wolf for himself, and while this boy is young, I know he's not innocent. He's a rogue alpha, one who is fierce and dangerous. One who could turn on me in two seconds flat. I can't forget that.

"*Pride-*"

I cut him off and level him with a glare. "*It's fine.*"

"*Look, why don't we-*"

My anger flares once again and my breath turns to fog in

front of my muzzle as I let loose a ragged howl. *"There is no 'we'."* I don't like the way he's trying to put me at ease. It makes me uncomfortable and suspicious. Needing a defense against his alpha charm I do the one thing I do best.

I harden myself.

*"I'm trying to think of our survival,"* he volunteers.

*"And survival involves us stopping to take in the view?"* I return.

Now that we've stopped, my muscles begin to ache from the hard climb and my body urges me to rest. But I don't want him to see any sign of weakness in me so I angle my head and try to appear unaffected from that long run. The last thing Logan needs to see is the depth of my exhaustion. I suspect, however, that my emotions are as transparent as cling wrap to this astute wolf.

*"We're stopping because I spotted a small cave over there and it's a good place to hunker down for the night."*

As my body screams for rest, I know I'm too exhausted to keep running, but ask the question anyway. *"Shouldn't we be looking for food, water, supplies?"*

*"There's not much more we can do tonight and I don't know about you but I need the rest."*

I stare at his hard body and as I take in his long sleek muscles, I know he's lying. He's barely winded and hasn't even broken a sweat yet. But then I realize what he's really doing. He knows I'm tired but understands I'm not about to admit it, so he's taking one for the team. His chivalry simply arouses my suspicion.

When thunder rumbles in the distance, he says, *"Come on, let's get inside."*

*"I'm not sleeping in that cave with you,"* I announce, partly because I don't trust him and partly because when a wolf slumbers they take on their human form. I'd rather not

hunker down in a small cavern with him, considering I have no clothes to cover myself.

He looks at me for a moment and I brace myself for a fight.

*"Fine, you take the cave and I'll seek shelter under those trees over there."*

Since I fully expected him to argue, his easy-going nature stops me cold. The men from my compound—wolves included—are dominant and forceful and are used to getting what they want.

There is a moment of strained silence between us then I say, *"You found the cave, you take it. I'll take the trees."* I offer him my back and step toward the makeshift shelter.

*"Pride,"* he says, clearly frustrated by my lack of female obedience and when he pauses I can tell he's trying to change tactics.

*"I insist,"* I answer, my tone letting him know the matter is no longer up for debate.

He pounces in front of me and his voice takes on a hard edge when he says, *"What's your problem, Pride?"*

*"I don't have a problem."*

He growls low and deep. *"Did you ever stop to think that we might need to rely on each other if we want to make it out of here alive?"*

*"I don't need anyone,"* I counter, but as soon as the words enter my thoughts, I'm reminded of my mother, my father, the elders. As bone deep loneliness rips through me, I suddenly feel like I'm going to cry. But I've desensitized for so long now, the tears don't come.

His face softens and there is something in the way he says, *"Everyone needs someone,"* that reminds me of a little lost boy.

*"I'm not everyone,"* I shoot back, wanting to anger him so he'll harden himself again. Hard I can handle. Hard I understand.

He nuzzles me with his snout, the same way the pups do when they want to play. *"Pride..."*

I jerk away. *"Don't touch me."*

He inches back and the wounded look on his face causes the strangest sensation to erupt in my stomach. I shudder, almost violently.

*"We'll hunt in the morning,"* I say for lack of anything else as I squash those strange sensations. I call back my anger because it's an emotion I'm more comfortable with.

*"Pride."*

I look over my shoulder, and I'm so tired I can almost feel the fight drain out of me. *"What?"*

His pewter eyes rake over my damaged body and his voice is soft when he whispers, *"I'm not going to hurt you."*

*"Maybe you're the one who should be worrying about me hurting you,"* I respond, distrust heavy in my tone.

With the tension between us palpable, the fur along his back bristles, and his silver eyes narrow. *"Do you want to hurt me, Pride?"*

Weary and with no desire to continue this conversation, I say, *"I don't even know you, Logan."*

We exchange a long glance then he breaks the silence by asking, *"What do you want to know?"* But I don't miss the slight edge that enters his voice; he can't hide that from my trained ears. It's that edge that speaks volumes and has alarm bells jangling in the back of my brain.

I'm good at reading people so I take a moment to study his body language. I note the way he's suddenly avoiding direct eye contact with me, an indication that he's keeping something from me. Clearly this alpha is harboring secrets and plenty of them.

*"Nothing."*

A few short hours ago I might have wanted to know things about him, things like where he came from, how he escaped, and how he gained the knowledge and dexterity to remove our microchips. After all, knowledge is power and I'm all about power.

But now, well, now that I've run with him, and noted his ability to distract me without even trying, I'm not so sure I want to know any of those things. And I can't forget the fear in my master's eyes when he first summoned me for this hunt. Maybe the less I know about this alpha the better.

*"Nothing?"* he balks. *"Come on, you must want to know something."*

*"If you're looking for a friend, or a mate, you picked the wrong wolf,"* I say, hoping my harsh words will silence him once and for all. All I want to do is escape those hunting us so I can keep the promise I made to myself.

Desperate to get away from him, but also desperate for rest, I walk toward the cluster of trees. Wind bites at my face and rustles my tawny fur as I look for a dry place to flop. I kick damp leaves around my makeshift bed and even though I've roughed it before, I can't help but think that maybe this wasn't my best move. Maybe I shouldn't have insisted that he sleep in the cave. But I couldn't bring myself to switch places, and despite the cold, bitter air, I'm not about to go crawling in there with my tail between my legs.

Off in the distance a howl serrates the night. I glance up and take in the angle of the waxing moon. With sunup still a long way off, I decide to grab a few hours rest before I flee. Despite my exhaustion there is no way I'm going to let myself fall asleep, not with an unpredictable wolf slumbering a few feet away. Besides, with the harsh elements nipping at my body, I'll need my fur to keep me warm. Once my wolf is well rested, I'll sneak away under the cover of darkness.

*"Sleep well."*

The roughness in his voice cuts through the night as he moves deeper into the shadows, to where he can't see me. I blink into the night and narrow my focus as I watch him grab a few big leaves for cover and shift back to his human body.

A fine shiver licks up my spine when I catch sight of his hard body as he moves with graceful ease. Raindrops play down his back and glisten on his skin before he ducks into the dry cavern, which looks more like a crevice in the rocks than any cave I've ever seen.

As my pulse pounds at the base of my neck I swallow, completely unnerved by my reactions to him. There is no denying that he's a beautiful wolf and an even more beautiful boy, which has me thinking of my own training.

A pretty face and good grace go a long way for two trained killers like us. It makes leading a mark and gaining their confidence that much easier.

Is it possible that this gorgeous alpha is using those skills on me? That he's trying to lead me somewhere?

Lure me?

Trap me?

I'm not sure, but as I drop to my knees and press myself into the rough timber, my gut tightens, warning me that it's well past time I made a run for it.

Too bad Logan has different ideas.

*ugust 26ᵗʰ Three days until full moon*

**I**n no time at all the bright morning light warms my body and pulls me from my deep slumber. My muscles cramp and my joints rebel as I stretch out my fatigued limbs.

As my body protests, my mind stirs and mixed memories of the long car ride, the PTF officers and the dangerous alpha wolf come rushing back in a roaring whoosh. My eyes fly open, my pulse quickens and my brain instantly kicks into high gear.

I dart a glance around and that's when I realize that I'm no longer outside, hunkered down beneath a cluster of towering oak trees, a safe distance from the boy who threatens me.

Panicked, I sit upright and my head cracks on something hard and unforgiving. I cringe as my fingers rake through my mussed hair to feel the beginnings of an egg size lump. Disoriented by my lack of bearings, confusion floods me and I rapidly blink my mind into focus. I take in my rocky shelter and vehemently struggle to figure out where I am.

My glance leaves the bumpy rock wall to trace my naked human body. I note the dry leaves covering my most private parts, as well as the weight of the strong arm curled protectively around my waist.

But it's who that arm belongs to that has a riot of emotions rocketing through me. A deep animal sound rises from my throat as understanding hits like a deadly bullet.

Despite my vow to stay awake, it's clear I drifted off, collapsing under the stress of the long, challenging day. And sometime through the night, when I was in my deepest slumber and unaware of Logan's intentions, he relocated me. He brought my naked body into his protected shelter and used the dual heat of our bare flesh to keep the frostbite at bay.

With his body pressed against mine, I squirm, uncomfortable with our closeness and the intimacy of his touch. As I take a moment to process this unexpected turn of events, I wonder why this dangerous alpha, who I've shown no kindness toward, would do such a thing.

I don't know whether to be grateful or angry but settle on angry because his gesture makes me feel vulnerable and exposed—things I never allow myself to feel. My heart thumps hard and as my hands go to my body to cover myself the sudden, urgent need to escape prompts me into action.

With my eyes trained on him, I scan his powerful body, and much to my alarm it stirs something deep inside me.

Something animalistic. Something primal.

But as anger mingles with these unwanted feelings I no longer see a boy, I see the hot-blooded hound lurking beneath, one who should have known better than to touch me. Fury overwhelms me and I struggle to keep my control, struggle not to kill this alpha who threatens all my emotions.

As my canines punch through my gums, I take a deep gulping breath and diligently force myself to calm down. Because when it comes right down to it, his gesture might have infuriated me— and confused my feelings—but he hasn't done anything so horrible that it would warrant his death, has he?

And contrary to what he might believe, we don't need each other to survive in the wild. I'm an excellent tracker, and deep in my gut I know I'm quite capable of negotiating the forest and warding off danger without him. With that last thought in mind, I make my move.

Still ensconced in his warm embrace, I try not to wake him as I carefully squirm out from beneath his tight hold. But he's nuzzled so close and the cave is so small it's hard to maneuver around his much larger frame.

I take extra care not to rouse him as I adjust my small body. I slowly, silently begin to inch away, but after a quick scan I know the only way out of the tight cave is to climb over him.

Logan makes a noise and his muscles flex and relax again as he shifts. I suck in a sharp breath and hold it until he settles.

With his head tossed to the side, his chest begins to rise and fall in a rhythmic pattern, and I wait a bit longer, to make sure he falls back into a deep sleep. Once he's stilled, I throw one leg over his hips, careful not to touch any other parts of his body.

Leaves cover him from the waist down and as I shuffle over him his scent reaches out to me. It's earthy and primitive and impossible to ignore. As I take in the hard lines of his profile as well as the muscles on his stomach, my wolf stirs, reacting to his animalistic scent and athletic body.

It's crazy how beautiful he is.

Shocked at how easily my wolf is distracted by Logan, I admonish her and concentrate on my one and only purpose. Escape. I move with predatory precision and crab walk over him.

Once I've cleared his body, I crawl from the cave, climb to my feet and sniff the early morning air for danger. As the scent of the forest comes to life after a long hard rain, a kaleidoscope of enticing aromas wash over me, everything from the moist, dewy earth, the indigenous foliage to the local wildlife that I can hear scampering about. It's all so clean, so pure, so rejuvenating. The warm sunshine even smells fresh and invigorating. My wolf growls as she feeds off the aromas, never having felt so alive.

A movement from the corner of my eye catches my attention and I spot a dark gray rabbit running through the underbrush. My stomach grumbles loudly. Soon I'll have to hunt and feed my hunger. But first I need to run and put as much distance as possible between me and the alpha before he wakes.

Just then a flock of noisy birds take to the sky overhead, their wings stirring the cool morning air as they search for food. I cringe and hope their high-pitched squeals haven't disturbed Logan.

Needing to flee, I scan the rough terrain and look for the route that will lead me to civilization. I know I can't go back the way I came, which means I have to trek north, and make my way across the wide expanse of park. As I think about traveling north I'm once again reminded of Canada and the compassionate packs of wolves who allegedly roam free.

Once I arrive at my destination, I'll have to find shelter and strategize my next move. Right now, however, I need to concentrate on surviving in these woods and steering clear of those brutal men who are hunting me.

I drop to the ground and moments before I'm about to shift and run, I spot a hiker's backpack near the tree. I still, and scan the area. When my glance comes up empty my mind settles on one logical conclusion. Sometime throughout the night, either before or after he placed my naked body in his shelter, Logan went hunting.

I steal a glance over my shoulder to ensure he's still asleep, then shuffle along the snow packed ground toward the pack. Ignoring the icy crystals beneath me, freezing my naked flesh, I crouch low, sniff the bag, and then with the utmost care peel the zipper open. I peek inside and when I find a change of dry clothes, panic invades my stomach. I slowly back away, not liking the direction my mind is taking me. My nape begins to tingle and my wolf tenses.

I have no idea who these supplies belong to or how Logan came upon them, but it does beg the question—did he kill someone in order to steal their provisions?

Deciding I'm not about to hang around to find out the details I breathe deep and call on my wolf, but a fine shiver moves through me to think how easily Logan could have killed me while I slept.

As my wolf emerges from my body, I bite my cheek to keep from crying out. Pain erupts inside me as my bones shift and my skin slides into place.

A few moments later, with my transformation complete, I immediately take to the woods, camouflaging myself in the thick timber. Legs pumping hard and a cool breeze ruffling my fur, I cut around the towering trees, distancing myself from the alpha dog as much as possible before he begins his day.

Ribbons of early morning light filter in through the thick canopy of leaves covering the forest and I realize that night is long behind me. As sunlight glints on my fur, I lecture myself for my carelessness. Exhaustion isn't an excuse for falling asleep and I know better than to run without the cover of darkness to veil me.

As the forest comes to life around me, I push forward long and hard until I come to an ice-capped summit. I canter to the slippery edge and glance down at the valley below. My stomach rumbles, reminding me of my hunger, and my dry mouth thirsts for water as I take in the lake and the thin skim of ice sparkling like a cluster of diamonds. The sight reminds me of my mating dress and has me thinking of Stone.

Now that I'm gone, Stone is the master's next best tracker. I'm sure the master will send him out to hunt me. I shudder at the thought of seeing the smug alpha again, but my wolf growls at the chance to fight him.

I recall Stone's distinctive scent and keep it at the forefront of my brain, because I fully expect him to come looking for me, to try to drag me back to the compound to be his devoted mate.

A shiver moves through me and I push that thought away. I turn my attention to the fog as it rises up from the valley floor. It clings to the treetops and obscures my view as I scan the rocky embankment and look for the best way down.

As I canter along the edge, my joints groan like an injured animal but this time I realize it's not from yesterday's hard run. I glance upward in time to see the moon disappear from the sky. A shiver of unease pulses in my blood as I count down the days until it's full.

My jaw tightens as I feel the savage pull of nature. Dark. Dangerous. Inescapable. I might be on the run, hiding from both the PTF and my handlers but as baser instincts call out to me, I realize I might have a more urgent problem at hand.

I know what my wolf can do. What she's capable of. And if I don't find a safe place to hide before the full moon I know what will happen to any unsuspecting backpackers hiking through the trails. I'm used to being locked up on shift night, the one and only night that I can't control my wolf.

Can't control her hunger.

I might kill for my master, but I don't kill for sport. It frightens me to think in a few short days, under the power of the moon, my bloodlust will take over. When that happens no one in this park will be safe, because no one will be able to tame the beast inside. Not even me.

With renewed purpose, I'm ever determined to find my way out of the forest, and seek shelter for my wolf. I take off down the side of the mountain, and keep my eyes open for both prey and predator. When I reach the valley below, I canter to the lake and stare at my bedraggled reflection as I take a generous sip of water.

As the sun rises higher, the layer of ice melts and I can see fish below the surface. My stomach growls louder and I take a tentative step into the water. I've never gone fishing before, but my wolf is swift. A sparkled fish swims by and I reach for it, but it proves too fast for me. I keep trying, again and again, but as the minutes tick by, I realize this is much harder than it looks.

Just as I'm about to give up and go find a rabbit, I hear twigs crunch behind me. I whirl around, fully expecting to find a hunter—or worse, Logan—but what I see instead has my lips peeling back to expose my canines.

Good God, I've never come up against anything so big before.

As my heart races in a mad cadence it suddenly occurs to me that I've only ever hunted humans. I've never gone up against an animal in the wild. I calm myself and try to remember everything I've ever learned about black bears.

I let loose a warning howl, but it does little to alarm the animal or send it scurrying back into the woods. It continues to move toward me with purpose, its sharp claws sinking into the ground.

When I snarl and spike my ruff the bear goes up on its back legs, its beefy front paws slashing the air. Its loud growl of distress lets me know I've invaded its hunting space, and it's far from happy.

I can smell its rage, its hunger and when I catch sight of a young cub coming out from behind a tree, I realize how much of a threat I pose to this mother bear, and how much trouble I'm really in.

Growling low in my throat, I keep eye contact and try not to provoke her into action. I take a small cautious step into the water, to avoid a direct attack. The last thing I want to do is hurt her. After all, she's merely a mother protecting her cub.

When the bear keeps coming I know I have two choices, run or fight. Although with the river at my back it really narrows it down to one choice. I crouch low and prepare to pounce.

I steady my breathing and when she closes the gap, I leap toward her, wanting to scare her, not kill her, but what I don't account for is her swinging paw, or the strength and power behind it. She catches me across the ribs and sends me hurtling backward.

I yelp as she delivers the bone crunching blow and land with a resounding thud a few feet away. As my head hits the ground, my sharp teeth gnash together and judging by the pain radiating down my neck I'm pretty sure I just blew my jaw out. Blood fills my mouth and my regenerative abilities kick in. My cracked bones begin to mend, and the pain ebbs as my jaw shifts and slides back into place.

I need a few more seconds for the healing process to finish, but I know I don't have them. I can hear her coming and can almost feel her hot breath slithering along my neck.

Blinking fast I diligently try to settle my shaken brain, knowing I have to clear the daze before she reaches me.

Pulse racing like mad, and self-preservation impulses surging inside me, I work to pull myself together. With my brain still wobbling, I try to climb to my shaky feet, to prepare a fearsome retaliation, but when a ferocious howl echoes off the mountains I almost sob with relief.

*Logan.*

I scent the air and catch a whiff of his fur long before I see him. I give an animal cry to let him know where I am and that I'm in danger.

Moving like a true predator he jumps from a nearby ridge and positions his body between me and the bear. Angry fire lights his pewter eyes as he gives a quick glance over his shoulder to assess my damages.

*"You okay?"*

After I give a quick nod Logan turns his attention back to the bear, which is suddenly down on all fours and dashing toward us. Like a fierce hunter, Logan begins to circle, keeping a wide berth as he draws her away from me. As I watch him and take in his calculating gaze and powerful body I shiver, fully aware that he's far more skilled than any wolf I've ever known.

Once Logan has her away from the water, his wolf barks a warning to me, to run for cover, but I'm not about to flee and let him face the threat alone.

Instead of running, I distract the bear by slapping the water. When she tosses her head and turns toward me, Logan uses that opportunity to go for her hind legs.

The bear growls and swipes at him, but Logan proves too fast, too strong. Within seconds he's airborne and with predatory accuracy he drives straight for the bear's throat. Sharp canines clamp down on the animal's neck and he quickly wrestles her to the ground. The animal drops and Logan's jaw tightens in a death grip.

Fierce and ferocious, he tosses his head, ripping into its flesh with primal hunger. The tangy scent of animal blood reaches my nostrils. As it spills from the bear's throat and turns the thin skim of snow a striking shade of red, my wolf growls. The delicious scent stirs my hunger and urges me to join in the feast. I climb to my feet, but when I see the cub, it snaps me back to reality.

*"Logan. Stop,"* I bark out.

He looks at me, stunned, then slowly backs away from the writhing animal. The mother bear growls, climbs to her feet and dashes off with her baby. As she leaves a bright trail of crimson behind, I wince and pray that no permanent damage has been done.

Dark splotches of blood stain Logan's muzzle as he comes toward me. His shrewd eyes look over my body and I know what he's going to say. I harden myself, prepare for the backlash, prepare to be humiliated for my overconfident attitude, because the truth is, out here in the wilderness I'm completely out of my element. Surviving by myself in this foreign territory is much harder than I anticipated.

Silence hangs heavy as he watches me, then something in his expression changes. While his voice is light I can still see the strain in his eyes when he says, *"What, you had to hunt the biggest thing in the forest?"*

I stare at him, and realize how close I was to getting us both killed. Logan might be a powerful alpha but he's just a boy and doesn't deserve to die because of me.

Not at all sure how to react I do the one thing that comes natural to me. *"Just so you know I had everything under control before you went all alpha on me,"* I shoot back.

Judging by the knowing look on his face, he isn't buying

my lie. His glance slides over me and he takes in my features until I begin to fidget under his watchful gaze.

There is a note of softness in his voice when he breaks the quiet and says, *"I know, Pride. I know."*

I gulp air. What I expected from him was fury, but what I get instead is way more than I can handle right now. The combination of his softness and the aftershock of the bear attack have me trembling like a scared kitten. I begin to shake all over. The truth is I never felt so scared, so out of control.

So completely and utterly out of my league.

I work to push down the panic rising in my throat and go down on my haunches, needing a minute to regroup. I steal a glance at Logan and hope he can't taste my fear as it hovers around us like a dark rain cloud.

His eyes glint knowingly but he doesn't say anything, doesn't try to comfort me. While I'm grateful for his distance, I really hate how well he can read me. I also hate that I spent my whole life building walls and with one simple look, one simple heroic act that happened to save my hide, this boy is able to puncture a hole in my armor.

As I take deep fueling breaths and work to get myself under control Logan's eyes zero in on my ribs, and the blood trickling over my fur. He growls low and a tortured look moves over his face.

His voice is hard and demanding when he says, *"I need you to heal yourself, Pride. Right now."*

With that, he turns around and shifts into his human form. He grabs the backpack from the rocky embankment and slides the zipper open. My eyes never leave him as he pulls on a pair of pants, t-shirt, jacket and boots. Once dressed he moves toward me with a pile of clothes in his hands.

He drops them in front of me, but I don't shift back. Not

right away. Not with his eyes still trained on me. I realize that with all that's going on back at the compound, and with life and death hanging in the balance out here in the wild, my nudity seems like such a foolish thing to worry about, but I can't seem to help myself. I'm a runt, one who is scarred and flawed and completely self-conscious around this alpha.

Just then a thick cloud moves in front of the early morning sun. As it darkens the forest, as well as my mood, Logan turns from me and makes his way to the water to wash up.

I want to thank him—for saving me from the bear, for the warm clothes, and for sheltering me last night—but I can't seem to push the words past my lips. With his back to me, he cleans himself up and I use that opportunity to shift and pull on the warm clothes at my feet.

"They're hunting wolves so I think it might be in our best interest to keep our human forms." He angles his head to look at me and the instant our eyes meet and lock I realize everything between us has changed. From here on out, whether I like it or not, we're in this game of survival together.

An uneasy truce has been made.

Unnerved by that thought, I narrow my eyes and ask, "Who are you?"

$$8$$

Logan stands and stares at me. "I thought you didn't want to know anything about me."

I roll one shoulder and try for casual. "If we're going to run together I guess I should probably know a few things about you." I stop to pull a few twigs from my hair before I add, "You know, so we're able to read one another if we land in trouble."

It's a half-truth, because when it comes right down to it, if I'm going to run with this powerful alpha, I need to know everything about him. It's the only way I'll be able to determine what I'm up against.

Is he a wolf who would turn on me first chance?

Then again, is there any other kind?

While he's shown kindness by keeping me sheltered last night and by helping me fend off that vicious bear, the truth is, from the world we both come from, wolves only show kindness to others when something is wanted or needed.

Does Logan need something from me?

I push to my feet and leave my boots where Logan dropped them. I walk barefoot to the river and note the fine shiver trickling along my spine, warning me to be careful where this boy is concerned.

Going down on one knee I bend forward, cup my hands and take a good long drink, until my thirst is sated. Then I splash my face with the frigid water and rub the dirt and debris off my skin until my flesh is practically raw.

When I come up and wipe my mouth with the back of my hand, I find Logan watching me. He has that unreadable look on his face again, an expressionless mask that hides a lifetime of dark secrets.

"What do you want to know?" he asks, his blue eyes flickering over me.

I don't falter under his piercing gaze. In fact, I hold my ground, let my glance pan over our clothes, then focus back on him.

"I guess the first thing I want to know is where you got these."

"Hikers."

"These hikers, where are they now?" I ask cautiously, the implication clear in my tone.

As understanding flares in his eyes, he smirks. "So you think I'm a cold-blooded killer, then?"

"It's good to know who I'm running with."

He dips his head and he arches a questioning brow as his eyes move over my face. "Don't you think if I was going to kill you I would have done it by now?"

"Not necessarily."

Logan might have spared me while I slept but I don't believe that means I'm safe, or that in a few short days under the pull of the full moon he won't try to tear my head clear off my neck.

"Well if you must know, Pride," he says in a very matter-of-fact kind of way. "I had to do what I had to do so I stole the backpack while the group of hikers were sleeping." He rolls one broad shoulder. "They had enough supplies that they won't miss a few things."

I eye him skeptically. "So why'd you do it? Why'd you put yourself in danger by sneaking into a camp where there were so many hikers?"

"Like I said, I had to do what I had to do."

"Why not catch one backpacker alone on the trail?"

"There was no time," he says, and I can tell he's losing patience with me.

Regardless, I plant one hand on my hip and glare at him.

Exhaling slowly, he pushes his hair off his forehead. "You're really not going to let this go are you?"

"No."

"Fine. It's as simple as this, Pride. You needed clothes, so I got them for you."

"It could have waited," I challenge.

"No. It couldn't have," he shoots back, then pauses long enough to slide a glance over me. "Because you're completely uncomfortable in your bare skin."

I blow an exasperated breath. "Unlike you," I rush out, unsure if I'm more rattled by his perceptions, or the fact that he treats me like a girl, not a wolf.

His grin turns coy. "That's right, Pride. I'm not at all uncomfortable with your bare skin."

My head jerks up. "That's not what I—"

Logan's bark of laughter cuts me off and I don't miss the way he skillfully redirects the conversation—putting an abrupt end to my probing—by saying, "Come on. I spotted a herd of deer not too far from here." He gives me a wink and jibes teasingly, "And while I appreciate you leaving our cozy shelter early this morning to go hunting, you know, so you could bring me back a big, juicy bear steak, I think perhaps we should stick to smaller game."

I ignore the crack and shove my feet into the warm boots,

which prove to be two sizes too big, but I'm not about to complain. I have a million other questions I want to ask, but as I tie my laces I can sense his reluctance. I don't need to read his thoughts to know he's being cautious with me, which confirms my theory that he is holding secrets. I suspect if I want answers I'm going to have to switch tactics and find another way to draw him out.

"What else do you have in there?" I ask.

He shoulders the huge backpack like the weight inside is insignificant, and in one fluid motion jumps onto the icy cliff. "A few staples."

Heading north we track back up the mountain in silence but as I follow from behind I keep an eye out for possible threats. I really don't want to come upon another unsuspecting bear, a mother who is simply protecting her cub.

When we reach the top of the summit Logan presses his finger to his lips and gestures with a nod. I follow his glance and my wolf stirs as the intoxicating scent of wild deer curls around me. It teases my hunger and there isn't a thing I can do to stop my stomach from rumbling.

Logan angles his head and lowers his voice low. "Do you want to get a fire going while I hunt or do you want to join me?"

I take a minute to entertain the idea. I've never hunted deer before and since I don't want to risk making a mistake and showcasing my flaws I lower my voice to match his and say, "I'll light a fire."

I turn to move but he grabs my elbow to stop me. He pulls me close and his scent practically overwhelms me when he puts his mouth close to my ear and says, "You're going to be here when I get back." I realize it isn't a question. It's a command.

Packaged in his arms, we exchange a look and when I stop to take his situation into consideration I realize he trusts me about as much as I trust him. Good. At least we both know where we stand.

I jerk my elbow from his hold and repeat, "I said I'll light a fire, so I'll light a fire."

His mouth tightens as he sizes me up for one more moment, then, astute wolf that he is, he says, "I guess you have a lot to learn out here. Once our stomachs are full, I'll teach you how to hunt wild game."

I snarl at him, wondering how this wolf can read me so well. Why am I so transparent to him? As I listen to the smooth, easy flow of his blood, I also wonder how a wolf who's also been confined knows so much more about the wild than I do.

Logan begins to shed his clothes and I look for a distraction. I shuffle along the ground and haphazardly kick dry leaves and tufts of moss out of my way. When I reach a clearing, a spot where the trees have thinned enough for me to light a fire, I gather twigs and branches and wait for Logan to finish morphing. Once he's transformed, I hurry back, gather his clothes, and take them to the clearing with me.

After I scent the air and determine that there is no danger lurking nearby, I make a rock circle, toss a few dry leaves into the pit, and top them with small, spindly pieces of timber. As I stare at my handiwork, I wonder if Logan has any tricks for lighting the wood.

Deciding to see what supplies he swiped from the hikers, I reach for the heavy backpack and pull it open. I rustle around inside the front compartment and when I find a plastic container filled with coffee crystals, I let loose a little joyous yelp. I open the container and take a long whiff. It's not hazelnut but it still smells delicious.

"I see you found the coffee."

I turn and as I watch Logan stalk toward me his strength and ability don't go unnoticed. Trying not to stare at his nakedness, I look past his shoulder and a few feet away I see a small deer. As I look over his kill, I can't help but admire his skill as a hunter. The scent of blood reaches my nostril and I pull it into my lungs.

My stomach growls and my nails extend, but I don't dare move. I know how things work in the wild and the last thing I want to do is provoke his wolf. Even my mother let my father eat first.

He cocks his head and asks, "Aren't you going to eat?"

"I thought the alpha went first?" I return.

Frowning he responds, "We're a new generation, Pride. We don't have to do things the way our parents did."

"I don't think—"

"Why don't we just eat together?"

I'm so ravenous that he doesn't have to ask me twice. Logan reaches into the backpack and pulls out a pack of matches. As he lights the fire, I turn away and shed my clothes. After I shift, we feast on the game and it's odd how I feel such a strange intimacy in the way we're sharing a meal together, probably because the alphas I know always eat alone and always go first. Logan moans and digs in harder. Since I don't know when our next meal will be I follow suit. We continue to eat long and hard and until our stomachs are bloated.

After we finish gorging Logan nudges me with his muzzle and says, *"How about that coffee?"*

I nod quickly and we both lope toward our clothes. We change back to human and dress, then I purse my lips and stare at the coffee grounds.

"How will we drink it?"

He gives me a look that suggests I'm dense, and I don't miss the mischief in his eyes. "You didn't think I'd steal coffee without cups to drink it in did you?"

"Of course not," I say like such a suggestion would be

ludicrous and when he points to another section of the bag, I reach in and pull out two small plastic cups. "That would be stupid of you."

His laugh curls around me and does the weirdest things to my insides. Not wanting to get too comfortable around this boy, I step back, putting a bit more distance between us.

"I'll get us some water." He opens yet another compartment and grabs a small pot.

"You really thought of everything haven't you?"

A crooked grin turns up the corner of his mouth, and I realize just how gorgeous he is when he jibes, "I'm a total bear without my caffeine."

I shiver, remembering the incident at the lake. "Then let's get this pot brewing because I've no desire to deal with another angry bear today."

I watch him go and conclude that if I have to run with an alpha, it might as well be one who is as fond of coffee as I am. When he dashes out of sight, I stoke the fire and wonder more about the boy who knows so much about survival.

A few minutes later he returns with the water and I scoop a few crystals into each cup as he holds the pot over the fire until it boils.

He fills our cups and keeping a safe distance from one another, we both sit back, lost in our own thoughts as we sip the brew. The taste instantly reminds me of Mica and my stomach squeezes. I stare at the sky and renew the vow I made to myself a few days ago, ever determined to get the elders out alive and crush my master once and for all. I don't know how, I don't know when, I only know it's something I have to do. But right now, before I can put a plan together, I have to figure out how to survive in these woods.

"Logan?"

"Yeah?"

"Why did you follow me?"

Suspicion flickers in his eyes. "Follow you?"

"Yeah, to the lake."

"Oh," he says and for a minute I wonder what he thought I meant. "These woods are dangerous, Pride. Especially for a wolf like you."

I can't help but feel a little insulted. "What do you mean a wolf like me?" I challenge.

"It's just…"

He pauses, like he's having a hard time pushing the next words past his lips, so as I grab a stick to poke the fire I come to his rescue by saying, "You mean because I'm a runt."

His head jerks up and surprise moves over his face. "What are you talking about?"

I wave my hand over my body. "You know, a runt. A genetic defect."

He grunts and a strange tormented look moves over his face. "You're anything but a genetic defect, Pride."

I shrug and ignore him. "I know what I am."

"What I mean is you might be a great tracker, but you've been locked up for what, seventeen years?"

When I nod, he says, "Out here in the wild, you're inexperienced."

Since he opened the door, I decide to enter. "So how do you know so much about the wild? Who taught you?" I ask, carefully drawing him into conversation.

He takes a sip of his coffee before he explains, "Basically hunting is instinctive, but pups learn tricks and techniques from their parents."

Interest piqued and feeling like I might be getting somewhere with him, I lean forward. "So you weren't always confined then?"

"No, not always." He fidgets and his throat works as he takes another long pull from his cup. The movement is slight but my wolf picks up on his sudden unease. What is it that he doesn't want me to know?

"So your parents taught you?" I ask, prompting him to continue.

"Yeah, my dad taught me to how to stay downwind, how to look for weaknesses and how to approach from behind. If you want I can show you those things."

I know if I want to survive out here it would be wise to learn whatever I can and accept whatever skills he's willing to teach me. "I do."

There is real sadness in his eyes when he says, "My dad also taught me how to spot infection in a pack. We'll want to avoid diseased game."

Talking about his dad has me thinking of my own and sorrow that I never got to know him well saddens me. I was only a pup when the master removed him because he was becoming too powerful, too influential amongst the pack. I might have been young but to this day I still remember his scent, his voice, and everything he taught me.

"Is your dad still, you know..." I can't seem to bring myself to finish the sentence.

He shakes his head and when he says, "No. PTF." I get the sense he's sharing something very private with me, something very difficult.

I look at the ground. "I'm sorry."

"How about you, are your parents alive?"

"No." I reach for another stick and stir the dirt at my feet, and without conscious thought begin to draw a picture of the ocean. "My master."

We both go quiet and I want to ask him where he lived before capture and where he's headed now, but the next question comes from him.

His brow furrows in thought and when I realize he's

watching me draw, I scrub it away, not wanting to share that private part of me with this stranger.

"Why did they call you Pride?"

"Because I'm a runt."

"How is that—"

I cut him off and say, "Despite my deficiencies I was the only one in a litter of three to survive. I proved to have strong survival instincts so in my parents' eyes I was their pride and joy."

Even though that brings a smile to his face, as soon as the words leave my mouth I want to grab them back and swallow them whole. I'm not sure why we've fallen into such a deep conversation or why I'm telling him such private things. I don't want him to know anything about me and I want to be the one asking the questions, not answering them. I drain my cup and think perhaps the buzz from the coffee has managed to overstimulate me and make me careless.

I turn the conversation back to him. "Why did they call you Logan?"

"It means wisdom."

"Really?"

"Yeah," he says grinning like a mischievous kid. "That's why I know so much."

I give him a suspicious look and in response he simply offers me a playful smirk full of secrets. I get the distinct impression that Logan doesn't really mean wisdom, or that his smarts come from his name. Names are very important in the packs, so I'm not really sure why he would lie about the meaning of his. Unless it has something to do with the secrets he holds close. I wish I had Miss Kara's laptop so I could look it up.

We remain quiet for a long time and listen to the animals scurry about and the birds squawk overhead. Rays of sunshine filter down and warm my body. I turn my face to the sun to absorb the heat, but what I'd really like is a nice long shower to wash the forest from my skin.

"I like your name. It's pretty." His glance races over my small body, which is almost completely swallowed by the oversized clothes he snatched for me. His smile is warm, wolfish and it makes my wolf stir to life in response. "I think it suits you," he adds.

"You don't know anything about me," I blurt out, suddenly uncomfortable with the turn of conversation, not to mention the way he's looking me over. I dart a glance around the clearing, not wanting to talk anymore. "We should go."

"Good idea." Logan instantly starts packing our supplies. "We have a lot of ground to cover before nightfall and I still need to find us a tent."

"A tent?"

"Yeah. I'll have to jack one because I can't imagine we'll get lucky enough to stumble upon another cave." When he turns and catches the fraught look on my face, one I can't seem to cover, he questions, "You don't want to freeze to death out here, do you?"

No, I don't want to freeze to death but I don't want to snuggle up with this alpha and use our naked bodies to create heat either. My brain instantly recalls the way we woke up only a few short hours ago. As my wolf bristles and those memories stir all her senses, a soft, primal growl crawls out of my throat.

"You okay?" His brow furrows as he kicks debris on the fire to smother it.

As smoke billows upward, I watch it absently and say, "Define okay."

He angles his head. "What, you have issues with sleeping in a tent with me?" When I don't answer he says, "Come on, Pride. We slept together last night and you don't seem any worse for wear."

"We didn't *sleep* together."

"You know what I mean."

I scowl at him. "You shouldn't have moved me."

He throws his hands up in the air. "You would have frozen to death in your sleep."

"You still shouldn't have moved me."

"So what, dying is better than sleeping next to me?"

"Yes."

He gives a humorless laugh. "You're really something, Pride."

"So are you," I shoot back, because this alpha is unlike any other wolf I've ever met. With a simple smile he has the ability to stir my senses and rattle my focus. That in turn means this boy threatens my very survival.

After this morning's attack I'm smart enough to know that without him I can't make it out of here alive. But the real question is, can I make it out of here alive with him?

ugust 27<sup>th.</sup> *Two days until full moon*

**W**e continue to head north, and for the most part we walk in silence, the quiet broken only when Logan stops to point out the difference between edible berries and ones that will make me violently ill.

As we pick a few along the way and fill our stomachs, he also talks about plants. He distinguishes between the poisonous and the ones that hold healing properties.

With my thirst for knowledge and my desire to survive in the wild, I can't deny that I'm enjoying his science lessons. I pay close attention, absorbing and hanging on his every word. I store the information and memorize the foliage because deep in my gut I can't help but think there is going to come a time when I might need to draw on it.

Continuing through the dense forest, we keep off the main path and push on for hours, until blisters form on my feet, and a sticky layer of sweat coats my body. I ignore the discomfort and continue my forward trek, shoving low-hanging tree branches out of my way and keeping an eye out for possible traps.

As I move through the trees quickly, my footfall silent on the rough terrain, I turn to catch sight of Logan. He appears to be having a hard time negotiating the forest in his human form. The way he twists and turns and ducks and bends around the low hanging limbs is almost laughable. Although, judging by the few curse words I hear him mumble under his breath, he doesn't seem to be finding humor in it like I do.

Off in the distance a noise reverberates off the mountain and when I come to a halt Logan nearly crashes into me. His body presses against mine and a shiver of awareness trickles down my spine. I suck in a sharp breath and hold it, my ears perked for movement.

"It's a long way off," he whispers from behind, but I scan the forest to be sure and try not to think about the way his breath is causing the fine hairs on my nape to tingle.

After deciding the noise is coming from some hikers we spotted about over hour ago, and not hunters, I allow myself to relax a little. I'm not sure if it's the same group Logan stole from and I'm not about to stick around to find out.

"Let's move," Logan says his thoughts obviously running in the same direction as mine. Even though we're off the beaten path their too-close proximity prompts us to move quicker. I'm just grateful that so far we've been able to avoid any direct threats, or contact with other people.

I stifle a yawn as day bleeds to night, and as the near full moon rises higher in the sky I calm my restless wolf and try not to think about what will happen in a few short days. As I fight down a pang of unease, I turn to Logan who still seems lost in his own thoughts.

I take a moment to assess him, and while his athletic body

doesn't appear to be tired or winded, I want to do my share of the work so I ask, "Do you want me to carry the bag for a while?"

He shakes his head. "It's light, but we should probably start thinking about sheltering down soon."

"We don't have a tent."

He sniffs the air. "I'll track back to where I heard those hikers." He points to a cluster of trees. "Why don't you rest for a minute and get a fire going. I won't be long."

"Do you want me to come?" Still uneasy after the events of the day a chill scurries up my spine, and suddenly I don't want to be left all alone out here, doused in darkness with danger all around me.

"No. It will draw less attention if only one of us goes. Besides, I need you to set up camp and keep watch over our supplies."

Not wanting to press, or show any signs of fear I nod then take the bag from him—which is by no means light—and work to push down the anxious feeling invading my stomach. I remind myself that I'm a strong wolf, a survivor, and I'm not going to let one bear attack shatter my confidence. As I diligently try to gather my composure, I walk to the trees and drop the bag with an undignified thud.

As Logan darts off in the dark, I settle myself on a tree stump and peel off my boots. Wet socks stick to my oozing blisters, and I take extra care to remove them. Cringing, I examine my sores as I drape the wet socks over a rock. A cool breeze tickles my toes as I stretch my legs out and drag the backpack closer to me.

I pull out the matches and with my goal to get my clothes dry before I have to climb back into them, rustle around the ground to find enough sticks to light a fire.

I think about morphing into wolf to heal my feet, but with the full moon so close I quickly decide against it. Hikers are nearby and I don't want to do anything to provoke her into action or taunt her hunger.

After I get a good blazing fire going, I grab the pot and decide to go find some water. Now that I've stopped moving I can feel a chill in my bones and could use something hot to drink. I'm sure Logan would enjoy a cup, too. That last thought stops me in my tracks. Disconcerted, I remind myself that we're simply running together for one reason and one reason only. Survival. He is not my friend.

I slip away but when I can't find water, I gather fresh snow and fill the pot. As I head back to the shelter I think more about Logan, and how he's able to seep under my skin without even trying. But thinking about Logan has me missing things I shouldn't have missed.

When I round the large oak tree, my skin prickles in warning and my steps automatically slow. I peer into the dark and what I see instantly snaps my attention back to the present and has my survival instincts kicking into full gear.

Startled, I step back, and hold my breath when I come down on a soft twig. I wait for the thin piece of wood to snap, to give away my coordinates, but fortunately, I'm light on my feet and don't weigh enough to break it. Once I'm out of the clearing, I press my back against the scratchy bark and camouflage my body in the shadows. As the scent of the hunters reaches my nostrils, my ears perk and I listen to their exchange.

"Do you think it's them?"

"I don't know. Let's wait until they come back. They can't be gone too far."

With the utmost care I begin to retreat, but when I hear leaves crunching behind, I stiffen. I prepare to turn, to attack, but a big hand closes over my mouth to silence me. As my body crashes hard against a rock solid chest, I let my canines push through my gums, ready to bite through my assailant's hand. But when I catch hold of his scent I nearly howl with relief.

"It's okay, Pride. It's me."

As my heart crashes against my ribs, I nod and Logan eases his hand away. He puts his mouth closer to my ear and whispers. "We need to go."

We back away slowly and once we've put enough distance between us and the men we can only assume are officers we turn and bolt. Even though I'm tired, the adrenaline pumping through my veins gives me a fresh burst of speed. We cut through the trees and run until we reach the other side of the mountain. Once we're well out of sight, we stop to catch our breaths.

Logan grimaces as he looks at me. "You okay?"

I lean forward, brace my hands on my knees and take a moment to scold myself. "I should have heard them coming."

"Don't be too hard on yourself, Pride. These guys are professionals and know how to close in."

I shake my head and dart him a quick glance. "What if I'd still been sitting there?"

"Then you would have smelled them and escaped before they reached you. Or you would have shifted and killed them."

"They have silver, Logan." I stop to shiver. "They could easily have stopped me." I pause for a minute and think. At least it was the PTF and not another tracker, because death would be preferable to the master's demands. At the thoughts of my master and what he wants me to do with Stone an angry tremble moves through me.

"I can't do what he wants me to do. I just can't." I whisper under my breath before I can stop myself.

Logan opens his mouth like he wants to say something but then seems to change his mind.

"We're both tired, Pride."

My mussed hair whips across my face as I give a vicious shake of my head. "I won't let that happen again," I say. "I need to stay alive." What Logan doesn't understand is that I have a mission, and death will simply prevent me from accomplishing it.

Logan looks around to take in the mountainside. "At least they're not tracking us by scent."

Once again I think of Stone and my pulse leaps. "My master will put another tracker on us. I'm sure of it."

Logan stares at me for a moment then asks, "If he sends another tracker do you think he'll let you go? Let you take your freedom?"

I give another hard shake of my head. "No. He'll send Stone."

"Stone?"

"He'll never let me go."

"Why?"

I turn away and my gut clenches so hard I think I'm going to be sick.

"What is it?" Logan grabs my arm and turns me back to face him. "What do I need to know about this Stone?"

"He'll bring me back because he's been broken. He's the master's puppet and will happily do his bidding."

"And?" Logan studies me and his eyes harden as they move over my face. "What is it you're not telling me? What is it your master wants you to do?"

I draw in a heavy breath and as I let it out I say, "In two days I'm supposed to mate with Stone."

Logan's blue eyes widen as he lets loose a long slow whistle. "I see," he says as he looks past my shoulder, to some distant spot in the forest. I watch the muscles on his jaw tense when he says, "And I take it you don't like Stone."

"No. I don't."

"Yet your master is going to mate you with him anyway?"

"Yes."

"Why?"

"To tame me."

He gives me a perplexed look. "He thinks a mating will tame you?"

"No. He thinks puppies will." I feel a burst of anger but tamp it down before I say, "And believe me, I'm not going to bring a pup into this world and let it suffer at the hands of my master."

His voice drops to a whisper and understanding passes over his faces when he says, "I can see why you ran."

I look at him and when I see worry shadows beneath his eyes I turn the question on him. "Why did you run, Logan?"

"Because the opportunity presented itself." He shoots a glance and redirects the conversation. "Do you think Stone is out here, scenting you?"

"I'm not sure but can only guess he is. I haven't picked up any traces of him yet though."

"Good." He looks me over, and I don't miss the concern on his face. "At least the clothes you're wearing will help mask your scent."

"Not with the way I've been sweating in them."

"Then tomorrow I'll go shopping, to restock."

"What's your currency exchange?"

He grins is slow. "How about I let our suppliers live."

His predatory smile and the way he talks so callously about life and death elicits a shiver from deep within and reminds me I'm running with a dangerous wolf.

"I lost our supplies so I should be the one responsible to restock," I say.

Logan mistakes the shiver rocketing through me. He steps closer and the air around us charges as he runs his hands over my arms, using friction to create heat. His touch makes me feel strange and unbalanced.

"It's okay, Pride. It's a bump in the road, it's not the end of it."

As he cares for me, the way an alpha would care for his mate, my numb feet take that moment to throb and despite the pain I'm thankful for the distraction. I step back, severing the intimacy. I pull a face as I glance at my purple, blood-crusted toes.

"I lost my boots."

Logan winces when he sees the sad state my feet are in. He bends down and starts untying his boots. "Take mine."

"I'm not going to take your boots," I shoot back. "You need them."

"I won't need them tonight."

"Why?"

"Because I couldn't find us a tent, which means in order to stay warm, I'll have to call on my wolf."

I shrug and reach for my zipper. "Then I guess I won't need them either then."

Logan grabs my hand and stops me. When I look at him in confusion, he says, "No, there is no sense in us both staying awake. You sleep. I'll stay watch."

As I continue to stare at him, still unable to figure him out, or why he's being so nice to me, a cool breeze ruffles his hair and rich, Pacific blue eyes—eyes that promise freedom—reach out to me.

"We'll take turns," I say, hoping my voice isn't as shaky as my insides.

A long pause and then, "Fair enough."

With that settled we go to work on gathering sticks to make a lean-to against the rocky cliff. It might not keep us very warm, but at least it will protect us from the wind and keep us hidden from the hunters who are out on night patrol.

I stifle a yawn, and think about the coffee I left behind. Since Logan is taking first watch, I'm sure he could have used a cup right now. Once again I mentally kick myself for losing our supplies.

"You want to sleep first?" I ask.

"No, you go ahead."

I turn my head when he begins to strip, then gather his clothes and bring them with me into our tight shelter. A moment later Logan joins me in wolf form. I can't seem to take my eyes off his powerful streamlined body, and without conscious thought, I reach out to stroke his soft fur. His coat is much thicker than mine, more conditioned for living in the outdoors.

He nips at my hand and I quickly pull it back. I understand his message so I curl up in a ball and press myself against the nook in the rock. He wraps his large frame around me and using his large body as well as the warmth of his fur, he protects me from the harsh elements.

As I absorb his warmth, and burrow deeper into his body, I consider the turn of events and can't help but think how weird it feels to be here, protected by this strong alpha. Especially considering that last night I refused to sleep anywhere near him, only to wake up naked with his body practically wrapped around mine.

Once again my mind races, wanting to know more about this boy. As if he can sense my rambling thoughts he growls low in his throat, and nips at me again.

"Okay, okay," I say and growl back. I close my eyes and calm my erratic thoughts and although I know I should probably be thinking about how easily this skilled wolf can kill me in my sleep, I let myself drift off.

I don't know how long I slept, but when I open my eyes, I see long fingers of light filtering in through our shelter. I run my hand along Logan's back to get his attention. The fur along his spine bristles and he gives a soft growl as he lifts his head to look up at me.

Even though he can't understand what I'm saying in my human form, I frown and ask. "Why didn't you wake me?"

I crawl out from under him and turn my back. I can feel his eyes on my body as I shed my clothes and when I hear him make an agonized noise, a deep groan low in his wolf throat, I know he's looking at the scars marring the length of my spine.

Seconds before I morph, I feel him move in close. I shudder as he runs his muzzle over my flesh, his fur tickling my skin and shredding my defenses. His big beefy paws trail along my shoulder, going all the way to the small of my back, but his touch isn't meant to hurt, it's meant to soothe.

Completely rattled, I gulp air and when he lets loose a howl, I inch away and call on my wolf. Once my transformation is complete I gather my composure, turn to him and nip at his shoulder.

*"Okay, okay,"* he says trying to lighten my mood. *"Did you forget that* I'm *the alpha?"*

He shifts and as I look at the naked boy before me, all sinewy muscle and power, my heart gallops. Oh no, there is no way I could ever forget this boy is an alpha. As the warm, familiar scent of him fills my nostrils I gesture toward his clothes and force myself not to show a reaction as I take in his nakedness.

With the cool air biting his flesh, he hurries into his pants, sweater, and coat but when his glance meets mine again, I can see the deep lines beneath his eyes. My heart tightens when I realize how tired he is and I can't help but feel a little guilty for sleeping so long while he stayed awake to protect us.

I nip him again, and when he curls up, I snuggle down next to his body. When he puts his arm around me, a strange wave of warmth moves through me. I flinch, a little uncomfortable with the way he's holding me, but stay close enough to offer him my heat.

*"Get some rest, Logan,"* I growl and even though I know he can't hear me, I'm pretty sure he understands.

His eyes slip shut and a smile touches his mouth as he pulls me against him, anchoring my wolf body to his. This time I don't move and a few moments later I hear his soft breathing noises. Once he's asleep, my wolf senses go on high alert, listening for possible threats and enemies as Logan takes his turn to rest.

He doesn't sleep long, just enough to take the edge off and when he wakes, he spends a long time looking over my wolf. As he brushes down my matted fur, grooming it back into place, I can't help but think how horrible I must look, and how much I'd love to have a hot shower to clean myself up.

He speaks to me, but I don't know what he's saying, so I turn my back and shift into my human form. He stays quiet as I pull my clothes on and I can't help but feel a little awkward as he watches me dress.

"How do you feel?" I ask to break the profound silence, which is making me feel completely self-conscious.

"Good. You?"

"I could use a shower."

He laughs. "That makes two of us. Maybe we can find a lake after we go hunting."

As I think about hunting I bite the inside of my mouth to hide my unease. "Okay."

Logan takes off his boots and hands them to me. I get ready to protest but he cuts me off and says, "We'll take turns. Besides I have these socks to keep me warm."

I pull on the boots and we step outside. The mid morning sun shines down on us as we stretch out our stiff, overworked bodies. We instinctively understand each other as we exchange a look and knowing we both have a job to do, Logan sniffs the air for game while I sniff it for danger.

"Anything?" he asks.

"No, you?"

He gestures with his head. "Down there."

I take a step forward, but Logan stops me. "Why don't you tell me which direction the wind is coming from?"

I stick my tongue out and taste the air, understanding today's lesson has already begun. "That way," I say pointing west.

"Good. So we need to get downwind, so the animal doesn't smell us first."

"Right."

Walking quietly, we make our way around the towering trees, and before we reach a small clearing, I see a herd of deer grazing. My wolf yelps, eager to give chase.

We stop near a large tree, and Logan unzips his coat. "Look them over, and tell me which one we should go for."

Never having hunted wild game before, I spot the biggest, meatiest buck and while my wolf stirs restlessly, eager to go for the juiciest steak, I'm a hunter at heart so I point to the smaller one at the back of the pack. "That one."

Logan smiles and as I watch him remove his coat and shirt I feel like I passed some sort of test. "My dad would have liked you." I don't know why, but hearing him say that about his dad has me feeling all strange inside. Logan reaches for his pants and nods toward my clothes. "Get yourself ready."

As I move away from him and begin to peel my clothes off my body he says, "We attack from behind and go for the hind leg."

I run over the information. "I can do that."

"I'll be there with you, Pride, but I'm going to let you take the lead on this. It's the way my dad taught me."

I nod, hoping my bloodlust will guide my actions and I don't screw this up. Once I'm naked, I fold my clothes and place them near the tree before I shift. Logan is ready and waiting for me.

*"Let's go."*

My wolf growls and we stay low, crouching on our bellies as we carefully close the distance between us and the herd. Instincts sharpened, I let my wolf take over and inch toward the grazing animals, which so far seem oblivious to us. I zero in on the one I want, and when I see the flick of its white tail, I make a move toward it. Unfortunately, my wolf is so eager to take chase she doesn't notice the branch beneath her paws. As the sound cracks the quiet, the deer lifts its head, sniffs the air and signals the others before bolting.

When they begin to run, I dart from my position and take off after them. Advancing with purpose, my wolf growls low in her throat and continues to take chase, but when I go for the deer's ankle the animal changes direction. My teeth clash and I fly through the air. A moment later I land with a painful thud and my empty stomach growls as I watch the game dart away.

Logan comes up beside me and nudges me with his muzzle. *"You did good."*

*"No, I didn't,"* I shoot back, angered and embarrassed that I couldn't bring down one small deer. I jump to all fours and snarl at him. *"If I did good, we'd be feasting right now."*

Logan shakes his head, the pewter in his eyes darkening. *"I've never met a wolf who was so hard on herself."*

*"Then I guess I'm not like the other wolves you know,"* I remind him, because I hate failure, of any kind.

He goes down on his haunches and looks at me longer than is comfortable. *"You're right, Pride. You're not like any wolf I know."*

The fur along my back quivers when I hear something in

his voice, something that sounds deep, dark and edgy. He steps closer, until he's standing beside me. His fur brushes mine and I feel a quick flash of heat inside me.

As this alpha overwhelms my wolf, my thoughts cloud over and I quickly try shaking the fog away. I'm small and inexperienced and if I want to make it out here in this unforgiving terrain, I have to have all my wits about me.

*"What did I do wrong?"*

*"You didn't account for the deer's speed. It's easy to miscalculate on your first try. I bet you won't do it again."*

*"You're right, I won't."*

*"Just remember, you're smart and you're fast."* He gives me a hard nudge with his muzzle as if to make sure I'm listening. *"A girl like you should never be underestimated."*

Restless and edgy I play his words over in my head and consider how he always refers to me as a girl instead of a wolf. I give a quick flick of my tail as I turn and canter back to my clothes.

I realize that beating Stone in an obstacle course is one thing, but I'm smart enough to know that my sharp instincts will only take me so far. Out here in the wild, I really have a lot to learn. I stop to think and wonder how far I would have made it without Logan. I also begin to think that maybe I need this skilled alpha a lot more than he needs me.

So why would Logan want to keep an inexperienced runt around? Aren't I slowing him down?

*"Want to try again?"* he asks.

*"Yes,"* I say, and this time I vow to get it right.

$$10$$

S o much for getting it right.

After a day of hunting, our bodies are dirty, our clothes are torn and our stomachs are still grumbling from lack of real food.

As if sensing I've had enough for one day, Logan turns to me, eyes me carefully and says, "Let's pick some berries and go get a drink."

Discouraged and in a foul mood, I nod in agreement. I take my dark disposition to the placid lake and as I stare at my reflection, taking in my messed hair, the dark smudges on my face and the grime that will never come out of my skin, Logan disappears into the woods.

Despite the cold temperature, the water calls out to me and I'd like nothing better than to get naked and climb in. I long to shed these soiled, oversized clothes and scrub my flesh clean but I have no idea how long Logan will be gone. The last thing I want is for him to come back and catch me stark naked in the lake.

I dip my hands into the frigid water, splash my face, then smooth my long hair down. I work the knots out with my fingers and gingerly tuck it behind my ears. It's the least I can do to appear somewhat presentable, not that I'm trying to look presentable for anyone. I'm not. But it makes me feel a little more human and less animalistic.

After I finish grooming myself, I go back on my haunches, wrap my arms around my legs and listen to the forest noises around me. Animals scurry about and wind whistles a soft tune as it whips around the trees, carrying the fresh aroma of summer sunshine with it.

As I decipher the unfamiliar sounds and breathe in the invigorating scents, I try not to think about the emptiness mushrooming inside me, emptiness for food, and emptiness for those I call family.

Needing something familiar, I grab a small twig and scrape it through the dirt. As I sketch a picture of the ocean, I continue to sift through all the scents and keep my ears perked for danger. Out here in the wild any kind of carelessness will only get us killed. And if there is one thing I know, I have to stop letting my attention stray to the boy who both fascinates and impresses me with each passing minute.

It isn't long before I hear the snap of branches and lift my head at the sound. I don't need to turn to know it's Logan. I can feel his penetrating eyes on me as he comes closer and once again my body quakes in that familiar way it does when he's near. Fighting the urge to squirm, I square my shoulders and take a moment to gather myself.

When I don't turn, he questions, "How did you know it was me?"

Once again I feel like I'm being tested. I know after our uneasy truce we're supposed to have each other's backs and can't help but wonder if his uncertainty has something do with last night, and how close, due to my carelessness, those hunters actually came to finding us.

"You're not very stealthy," I blurt out to cover the sting I can't help but feel.

"I prefer to travel in wolf form."

I hear something in Logan's voice that I've never heard before. When I turn and see him frowning, I get the sense I've touched on a sore spot.

"I didn't mean—"

"It's okay." He briskly waves his hands over his frame and I hear a hint of embarrassment in his voice when he says. "It's this body. Sometimes it doesn't allow me to move the way I want. It can be awkward."

My heart gives an extra beat as I look him over and think his body is anything but awkward. Then I think of my own size, and how I wish I was bigger, and stronger, like him. I lower my head and scratch at the dirt with my stick.

"I know what you mean."

"Really?" he challenges as he hovers over me.

My head jerks up with a start and I watch the way his dark hair falls forward, shadowing his features. It makes him look both rugged and mysterious. His glance rakes over me and his frown deepens.

He drives one hand into his pocket. "How could you possibly know what I mean?"

I open my mouth to argue but he waves his other hand toward the trees and cuts me off. "You move through these woods like a ghost, Pride, whether you're in wolf form or human form. I wish I was so skilled."

I stare at him, dumbfounded. "Are you kidding me?"

"No. You're lucky you're small. Don't think I haven't noticed how your size gives you agility and allows you to do things I can't."

Humor lights his eyes and I watch, transfixed as he pulls his hair off his forehead to expose fresh scratches and dents. "Does this happen to you?"

A strange noise crawls out of my throat. It's not a laugh

because I don't know how to laugh, but it's as close to one as I've ever come.

"I hardly think a few bumps and bruises would make you want to be a runt."

He shakes his head. "I already told you you're not a runt." When I give him a dubious look he says, "Let me tell you what you are." He holds his hands out and starts counting on his fingers. "One, you're light on your feet, two you're able to hide easier than I can and three you can move through these woods like a lightning bolt. Unlike me, you're a much harder target."

As I think about that and recall the awkward way he trekked through the thick foliage, I feel something flourishing inside me, some strange sense of pleasure that I've never felt before.

I purse my lips and the tight knot I always carry around in my stomach loosens a tiny bit. My words come out low, soft spoken. "I guess I never thought of my size as an advantage before."

Logan drops onto one knee beside me. His glance collides with mine and there isn't a trace of humor left on his face when he says, "Pride, you're one of the smartest wolves I know and when you start thinking of your size as a strength instead of a weakness, you're going to be one heck of a formidable hunter." He stops to glance around. "Out here, sometimes it pays to be small."

I think of his strength and power, his ability to run without tiring and the control he has when taking down a deer. "Sometimes it pays to be big, too."

He grins. "I guess we make quite the team then, don't we?"

Instead of answering, I shrug. This pack of solidarity with an alpha I barely know makes me feel uncertain.

Logan sits next to me, cups my palm and sprinkles a

generous handful of big berries into the curve.

As my stomach grumbles, I toss a few into my mouth, and the sweet juice explodes on my tongue. Wide eyed, I turn to him. "What are these?"

"Wild blueberries."

"They're the best things I've ever tasted," I say through a mouthful as I toss in more and chew heartily.

Logan laughs at me as he munches on his own berries.

I glare at him, feeling self-conscious. "What's so funny?"

"Your teeth and tongue are blue."

I lean forward to see my reflection in the water. I crinkle my nose as I run my tongue over my stained lips. "That's attractive."

"Yes, it is. Very."

My heart leaps at the deep rumble I hear in his voice and as a shiver pulses in my blood, I work to steady myself.

I clear my throat. "Logan?"

"Yeah," he answers softly and shifts closer—close enough for me to feel the warm strength of his body.

I slide him a look. "Where are you headed?"

"We're headed north." He gestures to a distant spot. "Away from Port Angeles. I thought you knew that."

"No, what I mean is, where are *you* headed? Where are you going to go after we escape?"

"A place where I can run free." He turns the questions back on me. "Where are you going?"

I hate how he always manages to turn the conversation away from himself, but answer anyway. "I'm not sure." I pause for a moment and think about those still suffering at the hands of my master as I run my stick along the ground. "Back at the compound there was talk about these packs that run free in Canada." I lift my head and look at him, to gauge his reactions. "Do you think that's true?"

A look I can't identify moves over his face, but before he

gets a chance to answer we catch a strong scent of animal in the wind. It wafts before my nose and both my nostrils and hunger flare at the same time. Logan presses his fingers to his lips and gestures to a spot behind me. I turn to see two deer in the distance.

"What do you think?" he mouths the words to me.

"Nothing ventured, nothing gained," I say, my untrained wolf nipping at me to morph and take chase.

He gives me a wink. "That's my girl."

I want to open my mouth to tell him I'm not his girl, I'm not anyone's girl, but when he silences me, I press my lips together and say nothing.

My joints crack as I climb to my feet, and a few minutes later we're both dashing through the woods in wolf form. This time I'm unable to keep up with the alpha as he shows me his strength and stamina in his primal form.

The rest of the day is spent hunting, running, climbing and learning, and I know this is the way my wolf was meant to live. I feel alive, and vibrant and almost giddy inside.

Throughout the lessons I concentrate on Logan's voice. I listen carefully to his directions, learning tricks that were handed down to him by his father. Soon I'm lost in the day—in Logan—and I force myself to temporarily shelve my worries in order give him my full focus. As I work hard, I take pleasure in the hunt and enjoy the freedom in running with the alpha. I exercise both my mind and body and Logan teaches me all about wildlife survival.

Before I realize it, the day has slipped away and darkness is upon us. I must say that while I appreciated his survival lessons, I can't help but feel I've let Logan down. My wolf lacks Logan's calm steadiness. She is young, untrained, anxious and her youthful exuberance keeps scaring the game off. As I look at the powerful wolf stalking toward me I once again wonder why he bothers to even keep me around.

Wouldn't he be better off without me frightening his dinner away?

As those thoughts bounce around in my head and pull my attention, I veer away from Logan, and push through the trees until they thin out. With my mind preoccupied I miss a low hanging branch. Thorny fingers reach out to me, and slash through my fur. I flick my tongue and taste the warm rivulets of blood as they taint my tawny coat.

I'm about to take another step, but before my foot comes down Logan leaps out of nowhere and blocks my path. Standing before me, eyes feral, and lips peeled back, he pounces and I land on the unforgiving ground with a hard knock.

Belly up and pinned beneath his thick paws, I look up at him and my wolf makes a low guttural sound. As my heart races, I expose my canines and I can't help but think this is the moment—the moment when the big bad wolf finally turns on me.

He presses his nose to the open cut on my cheek before it has time to heal, and pulls the scent of my blood into his lungs. He lifts his head skyward and lets loose a long, agonized howl.

I'm not sure what suddenly prompted him to turn on me. Perhaps hunger has finally gotten the better of him. Or perhaps the scent of my blood caused his baser instincts to kick in.

Regardless of the reason, it's not in my nature to go down without a fight, and I haven't accepted death just yet. I attempt to struggle out from underneath him but he's so big and so strong I can't seem to gain any leverage. I do, however, manage to work one paw free and slash out at him, catching fur beneath my nails as my mother's words of warning come rushing back.

*Trust no one but family.*

The gouge doesn't seem to slow him a bit. Air rushes from my lungs as he flattens himself along the length of me, and secures my body beneath his. I extend my nails and angle my head to search for a weapon, ready to fight to the death if necessary, but that's when I see the bear trap. One I nearly stepped straight into. As understanding pushes back my rage, a low, distressed howl crawls out of my throat.

As I watch the gash on his face close, his warm crimson flesh mending beneath his black fur, chaos erupts inside me. I swallow, hard, because Logan doesn't deserve what I did to him. If not for his quick reactions, I could have lost a leg, or worse...

The pewter in his eyes bleeds into his inky black pupils and when he looks deep into my eyes, I get the sense that he can see past the fur, the eyes, the girl and see into my soul, and can see how damaged I really am. Feeling vulnerable and exposed my body trembles like a leaf in a wind-storm.

*"Hey,"* he says, shifting his body over mine to offer his warmth. *"I didn't mean to scare you."* As he stares down at me, I work to think, to breathe. *"Pride,"* he begins, his hurt apparent in his expression. *"I told you I'm not going to harm you. When are you going to start believing me?"*

Rattled, and feeling like I've betrayed him somehow, I give a savage shake of my head and instead of answering I blurt out, *"I shouldn't have missed that."*

*"Then why did you?"*

*"Because you..."*

*"Because I what?"*

We exchanged a look and then I try to back pedal. *"Never mind."* I push at him. *"Get off me."*

He doesn't get off, instead his body moves on top of mine and there is something about the weight of him pressing down on me that causes my senses to stir in the most primal way.

His muzzle is close to mine and I can feel his warm breath on my face, ruffling my fur. His paw goes to his cheek and his mood shifts. His tone is light and teasing when he says, *"For a small wolf, you're pretty badass."*

*"Don't forget it,"* I say, wanting to sound more confident than I feel.

Tortured eyes meet mine and he gives a slow shake of his head when he says, *"Oh no, I'd never forget it."*

Something that resembles need flashes in those rich pewter orbs of his, but I know I must be mistaken. I'm a runt, no match for an alpha like him. I push at him again, hating the direction my thoughts are taking me because no alpha wolf in his right mind would give a girl like me a second look.

I try to work my feet under his belly to shove him off, desperately needing to disentangle myself from him, but my efforts prove futile.

As he gives me a look I can't decipher, heat surges inside my body and there is nothing I can do to tamp down my sudden fever. My brain stalls. Good God, no one has ever looked at me like that before.

His eyes sweep over my features, slowly, leisurely, taking his time to drink me in, and I become very aware of the way my body is responding.

He gives a slow shake of his head and says, *"You really are one of a kind."*

Feeling completely flustered by his closeness, I force myself to breathe naturally as I push at him, not at all sure what is happening between us.

My heart thumps as he inches to the side to remove most of his weight but he still doesn't clear his body of mine. Our hind legs tangle and one heavy paw remains draped over me, holding me down.

A shooting star scuttles across the sky and just then the

near full moon slips behind a cloud, dousing the woods in darkness. As his pewter eyes penetrate the dark night, they settle on my muzzle and he makes a noise as he trails a gentle paw over my stomach. I shiver, not because he's touching me, but because of the way he's touching me—softly, gently.

Intimately.

As the forest closes in on us and the air ripples with his scent, I feel like I'm being pulled under, the prey of some magical alpha spell. Suddenly, time seems suspended and no one appears to exist out here in the wild except me, this alpha and this moment. My pulse pounds in my neck and as Logan zeroes in on it, I realize he knows what his closeness is doing to me.

I search for my voice, even though I'm not sure what I'm about to say. *"Logan-"* I begin, suddenly needing this moment to end as much as I need it to continue.

*"Tell me more about Stone,"* he says.

His question helps breaks the strange spell he seems to have over me and catches me by surprise.

*"What do you want to know?"*

*"Would he hurt you if he found you?"* Logan's paw goes from my stomach to the small scar at my collarbone. He tracks it lightly, carefully.

*"He could try,"* I say. With my breathing hampered, I work to keep the quiver from my voice as his intimate touch pushes me past my comfort zone.

That brings a smile to his face, but it's short lived. *"Has he ever—you know—touched you?"*

I shake my head. *"I don't like to be touched."*

*"But he's an alpha, and alphas can be..."* he pauses, and he seems to be searching for the right word.

*"Do you mean forceful?"*

His teeth clench and anger clouds his pewter eyes. *"Yeah."*

*"No."*

*"So you were going to be put in his cell during the full moon."*

I nod.

*"What would you have done?"*

My nostrils flare as a burst of anger moves through me. *"I would have fought him."*

*"Would you have won?"*

*"No."* I turn my head away.

*"It's okay, Pride."* He nudges me until I turn to face him. *"I'm not going to let anyone take you back. I promise."*

My body tightens and the genuine concern in his eyes becomes my undoing. I bite my tongue and my defenses crumble like the dry leaves beneath me as everything about this boy generates a need deep inside me.

A long moment passes between us, both lost in our thoughts, then in the softest voice he asks, *"If you were free, and if it wasn't with Stone, would you think about having a family?"*

*"I don't know. I've never been free, so I've never given it any thought."* I pause and remind myself that I wouldn't want to breed a genetic defect into any family. *"If I had to answer I'd say no."*

In a move so fast that it takes me by surprise Logan slides off me and climbs to all fours. His thick muscles shift as he gives a quick hard shake of his head and focuses on the forest. His face is dark and troubled and I'm not sure what I said to cause his sudden mood shift.

He stays quiet for a long moment as he stares past my shoulder. I see tension in his posture as his eyes search the dark, but I have no idea what he's searching for. Then he releases a heavy sigh and looks to the sky.

*"The moon is getting higher and we need supplies. Let's get moving."*

And just like that, I'm left staring at his back, unable to figure out what happened between us.

$$\bullet \ 11$$

After returning to our human forms we pull on our dirty clothes and Logan insists I wear the boots as we go searching for supplies. Silence encompasses us and we listen to the night sounds and quietly make our way through the forest.

Strides determined, we climb down the mountain and when we approach the valley floor we hear voices, music and laughter. Flames from a bonfire shoot to the sky and create a soft glow around us. The smell of smoke and something sweet reaches my nostrils. My stomach growls.

Logan turns to me. "Why don't you wait here and I'll go check it out."

"Are you sure I shouldn't come? I might be able to get in and out quicker than you."

He frowns. "No, I'd rather you stay here so you can keep an eye and ear out for hunters, okay?"

Before he goes I untie the boots. He makes a move to pull off his socks but I stop him.

"No, you take both. I need to air out my blisters, anyway."

He agrees without argument and as he slips into the

boots, I find a rock to sit on and fold my arms around myself to fight off a shiver. Although I believe the shiver has more to do with Logan and what he's doing to me rather than the situation we've found ourselves in.

Moments pass as I listen to the distant laughter, and a tight ache begins in my core. As I breathe in the sweet sugary scents wafting through the air, I can't deny there is a side of me that craves that kind of normalcy.

What would it be like to go to real school, to hang out with friends after class, and only take to the forest with my kind on run night? I think about my mother and how much she must have missed that life and how much she longed for me to have that kind of freedom.

As I sit there and wait, I scan the forest, but when I spot a movement in the near distance my senses go on high alert. I listen and watch for a long time, until the sound of feet shuffling across the fallen leaves reaches my ears.

When timber crunches loudly, and a boy's voice reaches out to me, I know the intruder is human. He's humming a song, and hardly trying to be quiet, which leads me to believe he's not a hunter—no hunter in his right mind would go thrashing through the woods the way this guy is. I scent the air and as I breathe deep, I listen to his blood rush through his body.

I jump from my seated position and prepare, my wolf waiting to be unleashed. A moment later a boy who looks around the same age as Logan walks from the woods. He has a bundle of wood in his arms and a flashlight tucked into his armpit.

When he sees me he jumps back and both his timber and flashlight topple to the ground.

"Christ," he curses, and clutches his chest like the scare has taken ten years off his life. He quickly gathers up his light and sweeps it over me. As his glance darts around, confusion flares in his eyes.

"What are you doing out here?" he asks.

I look him over. In comparison to Logan he's a bit shorter, and not quite as muscular. His brown hair is cropped, tapered around his ears, and his green eyes might look confused but they also look kind. My wolf doesn't sense danger, so she settles.

"What are *you* doing out here?" I ask in return.

He nods toward his group. "Gathering wood for our fire." Then his brow furrows, suspicion trickles along the deep grooves. "Are you alone?"

I open my mouth to answer, but don't get the chance. Logan steps up beside me and in a possessive move puts his arm around me and pulls me close. "No. She's with me."

I glance at him, startled by his sudden protective movement. I can feel his heart crashing hard against his chest and the muscles along his side ripple as he anchors me to him. As I absorb the warm strength of his body a shiver trickles down my spine. His closeness overwhelms me but in front of company I resist the urge to pull away.

The two boys take a minute to size each other up. Then the hiker's light turns back to me. He fans it over the ground and that's when he notices my bare feet.

He curses under his breath. "Don't tell me they ripped you off, too?"

"Yeah, they took everything," Logan says without missing a beat. I look at him and admire his ability to think so quickly on his feet.

"Everything?" The hiker's green eyes widen, and he looks almost frantic when he asks, "You're out here in the cold and you don't have any supplies?"

Logan unties the boots and hands them to me. "We've been sharing as we make our way out," he says.

"Unbelievable. We ran into another group who had a few things jacked, too." He shakes his head. "Man, you both need to do something before you get frostbite and lose a limb."

"We've been looking for a park ranger, but can't seem to find any."

The hiker lets loose a heavy sigh and looks around the dark forest. "There is nothing you can do tonight so you should probably come back to our camp. We have plenty of food and spare clothes. Come morning we'll help you both get out of here." He bends to gather his wood and I exchange an uneasy look with Logan before he drops to the ground to help him.

"The name's Taylor," he tosses over his shoulder as he grabs his light and shines it on the path.

"I'm Logan and my girlfriend here is Pride."

I start at that false statement and shoot a glance at Logan, but he keeps his eyes trained on Taylor and ignores me.

With his arms loaded with timber, Taylor steps ahead. "Follow me," he says and resumes his whistling as he tromps through the woods.

Logan grabs my arm to keep me a few steps back. We walk slowly and once we have enough distance between us, he turns concerned eyes on me.

"Pride," he whispers. I look at him and note his furrowed brow as well as the tiny specks of pewter dancing in a stormy sea of blue, an indication that his wolf is concerned.

My hackles rise. "Should we run?"

"No." His voice is firm, to showcase the seriousness of the situation, I suppose. "Right now with everyone hunting us, we're probably better off with a group of people. Our scents will mingle and dilute. Besides, no one expects us to socialize out here."

I nod, but I can tell there is something else bothering him. "What is it?"

"We can't act like enemies. It would seem suspicious."

"Okay," I agree.

"We're going to have to pretend we're boyfriend and girl-friend. It's only logical."

Since I've had no experience in that area I say, "I don't know how to do that." For a brief second, I let my mind drift and think about Logan with other girls. But when I do, I get a strange tightness in my chest so I quickly push that image out of my mind.

"Just follow my lead."

"Okay."

"I'm going to have to touch you."

We exchange a long look and I know what he's getting at.

"You can't flinch."

I step over a fallen log and hurry along the path. "I won't."

Logan uses his free hand to push a branch out of our way. "You're also going to have to pretend you like it."

I nod and as my blood rushes quicker, I suddenly wonder how much pretending I'll have to do. "I can pretend," I assure him.

As we get closer to the fire we pick up our pace to catch up to Taylor. He drops his lumber and steps up to the group who are all seated around the campfire.

He waves his hand behind him and says, "We have company."

Curious eyes turn on us and my entire body tenses. Logan drops his wood on top of the pile and grasps my hand. When he gives it a reassuring squeeze I force myself to relax.

"Looks like they had their things jacked as well. They're out here with no supplies."

Just then one of the girls jumps up from the log she'd been sitting on, her dark ponytail bouncing from side to side as she shakes her head. "You're kidding me." She puckers her lips and gives me a once over. "Look at you," she says, her voice laced with concern. "You're underdressed and a complete mess." She makes a tsking sound and grabs a blanket from her tent. Mumbling under her breath she says, "I'd really like to get my hands on the thieves who stole your gear."

Not really understanding their genuine kindness my heart crashes hard against my chest. And when this stranger comes to drape a heavy blanket over me, I'm speechless. She runs her hands up and down my arms to warm me and I try not to flinch at her touch.

"Hey pal, what size are you?" one of the boys asks.

"Twelve," Logan answers.

"Will an eleven do?"

"You bet they will." The boy tosses Logan a spare pair of boots and he drops to a rock to haul them on. "Thanks, man."

Once we're warmed, we sit around the fire and as I adjust myself on the log, Taylor does the introductions. I learn that the girl who jumped to my rescue is Andrea, and the boy who gave up his boots is Jack, her boyfriend. After we exchange pleasantries, Taylor introduces Danielle and Trey, Michael and Brittany, and then he introduces his own girlfriend, Janie. I try to remember the names, four couples in total, as I greet them all.

We get comfortably seated and Logan initiates conversation. There is something about the soft lilt of his voice, his alpha charm and the way he presents a calm demeanor that draws the hikers in and puts everyone at ease. I have no doubt if we were normal teens, Logan would be the most popular boy in high school.

"What are you all doing out here?" Logan asks as shrewd eyes size up each and every one of them.

Taylor grabs two beers from his cooler and says, "Having one last party before we all go off to college in a few days." He tosses the cans to Logan, who opens them and hands one to me.

I think about turning it down, but the look on Logan's face changes my mind. I smile to hide what I'm really feeling as the bitter scent stings my nose.

"Where do you all go?" I ask and take a small sip from the can in an attempt to fit in. As the amber liquid slides down my throat I try not to show a reaction.

"We're going all over," he explains, and I note the sadness in Andrea's face as she leans into Jack. I don't need to ask to know that they're going in separate directions.

As her sadness reaches out to me, curling around me like a heavy cloak, I find myself leaning into Logan. At first he seems surprised by the uncharacteristic gesture, but then he wraps his arm around me to offer his comfort, assuming I'm doing it merely for show.

When Andrea reaches for her beer can a flash of orange light from the blazing fire dances on her ring. As I stare at it, taking in the pretty diamond stone, it instantly reminds me of my mating dress. Unease moves through me as I think about the elders, the puppies.

When she notices my interest she looks at me and smiles. "Pretty isn't it?"

"It's gorgeous," I say to cover my sudden discomfort.

A smile lights her face and travels all the way to her big brown eyes as she holds it out in front of herself to examine.

"It's a promise ring. We're going to get married when we graduate college." She turns to Jack and they exchange a kiss.

"Get a room will you," one of the boys blurts out and everyone laughs.

As I stare at the diamond I can't help but think how much I long to be a normal girl, long to love someone, long to be loved, like Andrea. But I'm not a normal girl, I quickly remind myself. And I never will be.

"It's a small diamond," Jack says almost apologetically.

"Don't be silly. It's not small." Andrea wiggles her slim fingers. "It's perfect for my hand."

Jack shrugs it off and says, "But when I become rich and famous she's going to need a wheelbarrow to carry her engagement ring around."

With that everyone laughs and Jack turns his attention to us. "So what about you guys? You both off to university in a few days, too? Getting one last party in?"

Instincts take over and I lean toward the fire to warm myself as I recite my standard story. "No, I'm a junior at Olympic High and Logan is a senior. We were on a nature hike until our things got stolen." I smile at Logan and when I look at him expectantly, he takes the cue.

Logan winks at the group then growls as he plants a warm kiss on my cheek. His tone is light and conversational when he says, "Well actually we're just getting away from the parents to have a little...*quiet time*...if you know what I mean."

When the boys let loose a cheer and raise their drinks, I clue in to what Logan means by *quiet time*. My cheek burns where he kissed it and my spine quivers as I think about such an intimate act with this big bad alpha.

Taylor winks back. "Hell yeah, we know what you mean. And don't worry. I have a spare pup tent you two can borrow. Very small, if you know what I mean."

As I think about sleeping in such a confined space with Logan, my heart misses a beat, my stomach flutters strangely, and beads of sweat break out on my body.

A cool breeze fans the fire and the flames lick the sky. Needing to think of something else, I glance upward and take in the stars. Just then a low howl rents the air and everyone tenses.

"Hey did you hear about the wolves on the loose?" Taylor asks.

I lower my head and work a strip of bark free from our

makeshift bench as Logan plays it cool and says, "No, never heard."

"Yeah, we ran into some gaming officers who warned us. They also left us a card to call if we catch sight of them." He pulls out his phone and holds it up. "Not that we could get a signal out here."

"I'm sure it's nothing to worry about," Logan says and brushes it off, but I can feel his tension and hear the strain beneath his words. "They're probably more scared of us than we are of them."

As everyone nods in agreement, Taylor relaxes a bit and says, "Yeah, you're probably right."

Trey, a very nice looking boy with midnight shoulder-length hair and a somewhat stocky build reaches for a cooler. His voice is rich and deep when he says, "You guys must be hungry."

I inhale the lingering scents around me and despite the grumbling in my stomach I say, "We don't want to take your food."

"Don't worry. We have plenty."

When I offer him a grateful smile, his brown eyes widen and I get this strange vibe from him. He's not dangerous, but he has this hyper energy about him.

"How do hot dogs and s'mores sound?" he asks.

Hot dogs sound great but I've never had s'mores before. I wonder if that's the deliciously sweet smell that's been teasing my hunger.

"Sounds great," Logan answers in a possessive voice that I've never heard before. As Trey approaches, Logan shuffles closer to me, until our bodies are practically meshed together. I hear a low growl in his throat but can't figure out what's threatening him. Alpha or not, I jab him in the ribs to calm his wolf.

Trey grabs two long skewers and comes closer. He plunks

himself down beside me and passes out the sticks. Danielle, his gorgeous girlfriend who looks very much like the bubbly cheerleader type, reaches for another beer and I notice the way she wobbles slightly as she watches us from across the fire pit.

I place my can of beer on the ground beside me and Logan takes it and moves it to the other side of him. We exchange a knowing look and it becomes clear to me that with each passing moment we're getting better and better at reading each other.

Logan takes a small drink from his can, then when no one is looking pours the rest out. I guess he doesn't want to run the risk of lowering his inhibitions either because we need to keep awake and alert if we want to survive out here.

After we take our skewers, Trey tears open a new pack of hotdogs. He holds the package out and Logan grabs one to put on the end of his stick and as I'm about to follow suit, Trey closes his hand over mine.

"Here let me help you."

I'm quite capable of doing it myself but I don't want to offend anyone so I let him. He shifts a little closer to me and keeps his hand over mine. He pierces the hot dog and holds it over the fire.

While I cook my food the boys strike up conversation, but I don't miss the tension emanating off Logan as he watches Trey. If I didn't know better, I'd think he was about to shift and pounce. Something about Trey threatens his wolf, but I can't quite figure out what it is.

Keeping one eye on me, and the other on the group, Logan joins the conversation. The girls look bored as the guys talk about cars, recent movies, sports, and some ultimate fighting show they all watch on TV. As I listen, I'm not at all bored. What I am, however, is surprised by how much Logan knows. I'm also surprised by the possessiveness in his glance whenever he looks at me.

Once my hot dog is cooked, I begin to nibble on it, taking my time so I don't come off like a starved dog. When Danielle clears her throat loudly, Trey slinks back to her, leaving the package of hot dogs behind. Danielle speaks to her boyfriend in whispered words, but with my trained ears I'm able to hear them, and what I hear startles me.

*Flirting with me?*

Is that what she thinks he was doing? When hunting for my master, I've flirted with guys to gain their trust, but a guy has never flirted with me before. I turn to Logan, who has also been listening. He nods his head at me and he seems highly agitated when he whispers, "What you were sensing was his interest in you."

Before I can respond, Brittany, a pretty petite blonde, who appears to be the same size as me, jumps up and her green eyes are alive with laughter when she says, "Time for more s'mores."

"Haven't you eaten enough?" Janie asks, laughing. "Not that it matters, you skinny bitch." Then she rolls her blue eyes and turns them on me. "I suppose you can eat all you want and never put on a pound either."

I know she's teasing, but I'm not sure how to respond. Brittany comes to my rescue.

"Ignore her. She's been on a liquid diet and it's making her insane."

I look Janie over. She is tall, gorgeous, and curvy in all the right places. She's everything I'm not, everything I long to be. I frown, confused by such behavior. "Why would she be on a liquid diet?"

"Because she thinks she's fat," Brittany explains.

My eyes widen and before I can help myself I blurt out, "She's gorgeous."

"Okay, Pride, you're my very new best friend," Janie says and the girls all laugh.

Brittany steps behind Logan to grab another cooler. She pulls out supplies, hands them around and takes a seat next to him. She punctures her marshmallow, warms it over the flames then wraps it in chocolate and graham cracker.

As we watch her eat, Logan stabs a marshmallow with his skewer and follows her lead. Within seconds it goes up in a burst of flames. He pulls it away and tries to wrap it in chocolate, only to end up with a hot mess on his hands.

Everyone is laughing and I can't help but smile at him. This skilled hunter who can slay a deer with his bare hands and chase off a mother bear is actually having a hard time building a s'more, which smells so amazing that I'm ready to scarf it down without even bothering to cook the marshmallow.

When he hears me make a noise that resembles a laugh, he turns to me and runs his fingers over my face, coating me in chocolate. Everyone laughs harder and I stick my tongue out to taste the sweetness.

My stomach howls for more. That has to be the most delicious thing I've ever tasted. I look at Janie. Why she would deprive herself of this is beyond me. Then again, I've been caged my whole life and don't understand 'high school girl' way of thinking.

As Logan licks his fingers clean, I look around at the group. Everyone is having such a good time it has my heart swelling in my chest. Once again I'm reminded that the young teenage girl inside me wants this, wants the normalcy of it all. Friends. Camaraderie. Laughter.

But my gut reminds me of my mission. One I might not come back from. And I'd be smart to remember that emotions play no part in my game of survival. I sober at that last thought and Logan turns to me, sensing my mood shift.

Brittany drops next to him. Still laughing and genuinely sincere she shoves another marshmallow onto his stick and gives him directions as she holds it over the fire.

"Put the chocolate on the graham cracker and hold the sides open," she directs.

When Logan obliges, I watch Brittany lean close, her body is only inches from Logan's and the clean scent of her skin wafts before our nostrils. I think of my own body, and how filthy I must look in comparison, and for the first time in my life I feel the sting of something new, something that could be jealousy.

I take a deep breath, but can't seem to fill my lungs.

Needing escape, I climb to my feet. "I'm a mess," I say, in my most even voice. "I need to get washed up."

Brittany glances up at me. "We found a nice hot spring over that hill." She waves her hands in the direction. "It's beautiful and warm. You'll love it."

I turn to go but she says, "Wait, let me get you some clean clothes."

She comes back within seconds and hands me soap, sweat pants and a sweater. "These should fit. We look about the same size." I look her over and realize that she's small like me, but she doesn't look like a runt at all. She's cute, petite, and quite appealing. Is it possible that others see my runt body the same way?

"Thank you," I croak out.

"My pleasure, Pride."

With a knot in my stomach, I make a turn to go but Brittany stops me. I turn back to her. "Great name by the way."

I smile, think of my parents, and vow to live up to their expectations. "Thanks." With that I make my way to the hot springs, following her directions.

When I find it, I strip and wade out until I'm waist high. I give a soft sigh and scan the tree line, my senses always perked for danger. But the warm water feels so glorious on my body it's hard to concentrate. I spread my arms and watch the waves ripple around me, then using the soap, I begin to lather my grimy skin.

As I wash the dirt from my flesh, allowing the sweet jasmine scent to fill my nostrils, I get the sense someone is watching me. I turn and see Logan standing at the edge of the pool.

Gaze intense and pinned on me, his eyes glisten beneath the near full moon. My heart thumps fast as I watch him. He doesn't ask permission to join me. Instead he sheds his clothes and stalks closer. A moment later he's standing in front of me, and as our naked bodies almost touch I note there isn't a hint of shyness about him.

I begin to cover my flesh, but he captures my hands to stop me.

"Don't," he says, and the intensity in his voice frightens me as much as it excites me. "You have no reason to hide from me."

A lump lodges in my throat and I have to force my words past it. "Logan-"

"It's okay, Pride."

"Logan please..."

"Please what?"

"I don't want you to see me. I'm...I'm..."

"You're what?"

"I'm not like the others." I steal a quick glance at him and I know he can see right through me.

Anger moves over his face. "We all have scars."

"Not like mine," I finally say. "I'm not...right," I say, not quite knowing how to say what I really feel. That I'm damaged and unlovable.

"You're wrong, Pride. What you are is beautiful. Inside and out."

I turn away, no longer wanting to meet his eyes, no longer wanting him to see my body.

He takes hold of my elbow and turns me back to him. "Pride, you have nothing to be ashamed of. We're naked in our wolf form, so why does naked in our human form bother you?"

"I don't know," I manage to get out. "Being around you makes me so aware of my body."

"Your female body is beautiful, Pride." His voice drops an octave when he adds, "And if you want to know the truth, it makes me very aware, too."

I look at him and can hardly believe what he's saying. A deep, strangled sound rises from my throat. "Why are you doing this? Why are you being so nice to me?"

He trails a hand over my arm and takes a measured step closer. "Because we need each other."

"But you're an alpha. Alphas are never nice. They control and dominate. You even said so yourself."

"I have no reason to control or dominate you. I want us to be equals."

"Equals? How can we possibly be equals?" I ask.

He gives a slow shake of his head. "You have no idea how special you are, do you?"

My voice comes out a low strained whisper when I say, "You must be mistaking me for someone else."

"Oh, no, little one. Like I said before, there is no one else like you." His soft voice wraps around me and holds me so tight it does the weirdest things to my insides.

I feel his fingers on my flesh and as his hands trace my scars it produces an unfamiliar fullness in my chest. I shiver, completely unnerved by his touch. But oddly enough, this time I don't find myself shying away from it, this time I find myself leaning into it, needing it, absorbing it and letting it fuel me in the most unfathomable ways.

His hair falls forward as his eyes track my scars. Emotions move over his face and I wonder how this boy, this skilled hunter can be so ferocious in the wild yet be so soft and gentle with me.

"You're beautiful, Pride," he tells me again as he takes the soap from me to wash his own body. "Didn't you see the way those guys were looking at you?" A slow grin turns up the corner of his perfect mouth. "I thought I was going to have to go feral and fight them off."

A strange laugh rises in my throat. "I hardly think..." I begin, but my voice fails when he leans forward and presses his lips to the scars at the base of my neck. The warmth of his mouth burns my blood. I suck in a sharp breath and try not to explode into a million tiny pieces.

He traces my scar with his lips, the caress meant to soothe the years of pain. "No one is ever going to hurt you again," he growls under his breath and to illustrate his protectiveness he holds me tight. His glance moves over my face and specks of pewter dance in his eyes when he says, "If they try, they'll have to go through me."

A strange noise rumbles in my throat as I gaze at him. I take in the fierceness in his eyes, along with his vow to protect me, and in that instant it becomes glaringly apparent that everything between us has changed. A shudder races through me and there isn't a thing I can do to stop the small choking sound in my throat.

"Are you okay?" he asks.

"Not even a little," I answer honestly, my voice as shaky as my body.

"Come here." He pulls me impossibly closer, and hugs me to his body. Without conscious thought my arms circle his waist. His muscles feel hard beneath my hands and I realize it's the first time I've touched his human body. As his scent curls around me and draws me into a blanket of warmth my low howl breaks the quiet of the night.

He presses his nose into my hair and pulls in my scent as his fingers span the small of my back. This time I melt into him because I'm so shaken I can barely keep my legs from failing.

Everything in the way he touches me, and everything in the way he looks at me has shattered my last vestige of control and I know in this instant, life as I know it will never be the same again.

A moment later a branch cracks, breaking the spell, and we both tense. I turn in time to catch sight of a large raccoon as it darts into the underbrush.

Logan clears his throat, and puts his mouth close to my ear. My body tingles when he whispers, "We should get back. It's late and we need sleep."

Since I can't find my voice I simply nod. He captures my hand in his and stays near as he leads me out of the water. We dress in silence and I notice how close he stands to me as we make our way back to the camp. When I see the small pup tent set up especially for us, it occurs to me we'll be sleeping in tight quarters together—with both of us in our human form.

My entire body tightens in a way it has never tightened before and a warm shiver of awareness hurries down my spine.

I bite the inside of my mouth and slow my steps. As I stall I become acutely aware of the way Logan is watching me.

I'm suddenly not sure if I want to crawl into the tight intimate space with him. Not because I don't trust him, but because this time, I don't trust myself.

12

The murmured sounds of the hikers drift through the quiet night air as we all prepare for bed. Even though I'm pushed past my comfort zone, I try to act normal, try to pretend that crawling into bed with Logan is something I do on a regular basis. My insides, however, are in a complete uproar and the food I've eaten earlier has settled into a big chaotic lump in the pit of my stomach.

After we exchange 'good-nights' Logan holds the tent flaps open for me and I scurry inside. I leave my clothes on and struggle to keep my breathing steady as I climb between the sleeping bags. Pretending we're a couple, Logan crawls in with me. I look at the powerful, big bad alpha moving in beside me and can't help but think this is a dangerous game I'm playing.

My pulse pounds hard as I snuggle deeper into my pillow and when Logan shifts closer I can feel heat and strength radiating from him as he offers me his warmth. My entire body reacts to his close proximity and I almost feel dizzy.

I listen to Logan's soft breathing and hear his throat work as he swallows and I get the distinct impression that he is struggling to keep his composure, a difficult task for an alpha like him, I'm sure.

He puts an arm around me and when I turn into him, he pulls me in closer and I realize how nice it feels to be held by him. The earthy scent of his skin, so achingly familiar to me now, stirs my wolf and it takes all my effort not to let loose a distressed howl. My toes curl as my thoughts fragment.

"This is much better than last night," he says, and for the first time I hear something in his voice, something that makes me think he's as nervous as I am. He sinks deeper into the blankets. "Softer, too."

Logan touches my arm, and when I stiffen, still not used to the softness of his touch, he pulls his hand back like he's been burned. His glance flits over mine and I see a hint of uncertainty in his eyes before he rolls onto his back.

As I watch him, it reminds me that beneath that big bad alpha Logan is just a boy, and inside this tent, as nature compels us to do what comes naturally between a boy and a girl, he's just as uncertain as I am.

He crooks his elbow and braces one arm under his head. As I watch him stare skyward, I wonder what he's thinking.

"You tired?" I ask evenly, even though everything about this boy is playing havoc with my senses and rattling what little calm I can seem to muster.

"Yeah," he says, his voice coming out a little rough around the edges. "You?" He takes a deep breath and when he wets his lips my gaze lingers on the streak of moisture and I can't help but wonder what it would feel like to be kissed by him.

I bite back a breathy moan, suddenly terrified by what I'm feeling, and remember he's waiting for an answer. "Exhausted," I finally say.

He angles his head to see me and when he gives me the softest smile I've ever seen I nearly melt into the sleeping bag.

I think about the way he touched me tonight, the way he treated me like a girl, not an animal, and the way he made me feel proud and beautiful of myself just the way I am. I also think about the way he kissed my scars with the utmost care. A burst of heat rushes up my spine and I can feel my face flush hotly.

Flustered and completely unsure of myself, I pull the blanket up higher to hide my body's reactions. Logan turns into me and gathers a damp wayward strand of my hair between his fingers. He brings it to his nose and inhales.

"You smell good."

When I swallow, he leans closer and I wonder if he's about to make a move on me. As his glance races over my face he wets his lips again and I wonder if I'm finally going to know what it's like to be kissed.

My eyes widen and my heart pounds as equal mixtures of nervousness and excitement pulse inside me. Logan inhales and I know he can taste my tension. I just hope he doesn't mistake it for fear.

My fingers tingle and I want to touch him, to draw his mouth to mine, but I can't seem to move. It feels as if the connection between my brain and body has been completely disengaged and I'm left paralyzed—a perilous state for a wolf on the run to find herself in, especially one who is running with an alpha who holds secrets.

He opens his mouth like he wants to say something, and my blood is pounding so hard in my ears I'm sure I won't be able to hear him. When apprehension invades my stomach, dark, tortured emotions pass over his eyes and his nostrils flare.

A strange sense of disappointment runs through me when he rolls back over. I watch his chest rise and fall as he sucks in a ragged breath and I get the sense that he's fighting some sort of internal battle.

"Try to get some sleep, Pride," he says in a rusty voice full of torment. "I want to cover a lot of ground tomorrow."

As a barrage of emotions roll off his body, he looks skyward again, and my chest tightens so hard it's almost impossible to breathe.

Logan closes his eyes and suddenly all I want to do is climb from the tent and lose myself in the woods. My wolf cries, wanting to run, wanting to get as far away from Logan as possible. Everything about him rattles me, disarms me in a way that leaves me vulnerable.

Instead of bolting, I slam my lids shut and force myself to relax. I take a long time to sort things through then come to the realization that his retreat was for the best. I have a mission to concentrate on and don't need such complications.

I let my thoughts drift to the compound, and take that moment to berate myself for my behavior. People are being abused at the hands of a cruel man while I lay here in comfort and feel sorry for myself.

Disgusted by my selfishness, I push all thoughts of Logan aside and try to relax, knowing that in the upcoming days I'll need my strength.

Moments before I'm about to drift off a scent has my lids springing open. My blood rushes fast as my senses sort through the information. The second my brain deciphers exactly who the smell belongs to my heart begins to gallop. I breathe deep, but know I have to be wrong.

I just have to be.

I take a quick glance at Logan, who is sleeping restlessly beside me, then quietly crawl out of my covers. I peel the zipper open and pull the night air into my lungs.

A cry chokes in my throat as a queasy feeling blooms in my stomach. I swallow hard and moving with stealth I silently slip out of the tent. Climbing to my feet, I stand there for a moment and fight down a howl as I breathe in a scent that has my heart aching.

With emotions getting the better of me and before I have a chance to consider the consequences of my actions, I dart through the trees, my glance cutting from left to right as I peer into the dark night in search of my father.

But how can this be? How can my father still be alive?

I follow his scent until it grows stronger. My nose begins to tingle and when my eyes water I know he is close. So close.

I push a branch out of my way and take a step into the clearing. When I see a piece of cloth on the ground, one that holds my father's distinctive scent, my heart nearly stops. I take another small step and that's when my instincts react to danger a split second before my brain catches up.

But before I can leap a wire tightens around my ankle and lifts me clear off the ground. I struggle but the sharp wire snaps tight and my breath is torn from my lungs as I fly through the air. Dangling upside down, my back smacks against the tree trunk and the sound echoes around me. I bend at the waist and fight to loosen the restraint. Except the more I squirm the tighter it pulls.

As my mind races I think about shifting, but will the wire tear through the bone and sever my leg? I bite back a wounded cry, not wanting the hunters to know I've been snared in their trap, but the rustling in the woods warns it's too late.

Panicked, I'm about to shift and take my chances with the wire, but when I hear, "*Pride, don't,*" I dart a glance to my left in time to see Stone step from the darkness.

My heart slides into my throat and there is nothing I can do to keep the howl in my lungs.

"*Shh,*" he warns, speaking telepathically as he angles his head unnaturally, listening for something. Before I realize what he's doing, he pulls a knife from his pocket and walks toward me.

"*Back off,*" I warn between gritted teeth, and despite the wire chewing into my leg I try to swing my body. If I can reach the tree, maybe I can climb up.

As the coppery scent of my blood fills the air, Stone's nostrils flare and he says, "*If you want me to get you down you need to stay quiet and still.*"

"*You sure you want to do that?*" I challenge.

He cuts me a careful glance, and his voice lacks the hard bite I'm accustomed to when he says, "*Pride, please, I'm not going to hurt you.*"

"*Fine, I guess that will just make it easier for me to kill you then.*"

In that instant I see something in his expression, something dark and troubled. Something that instantly tells me there is more going on than I know.

His head lifts and he sniffs the air like a true predator, then shoots another glance around. His voice is low, conspiratorial when he says, "*Pride, you need to listen to me.*"

With impatience thrumming through me, I touch his thoughts. His eyes harden as I move past the chaos. As his tortured visions flood me, I gulp air. Once again I'm bombarded with numbers and hear a gun shot—has he had some fight that I have no knowledge of?

What is it I'm not grasping?

I try to puzzle it out, but when the chaos parts way and I see an image of me in my mating dress, rage races through me and I extricate myself from his mind.

"*I'll never be your mate.*"

He gives a hard shake of his head and his voice is grave when he says, "*Pride, you don't under-*"

Before he can finish the sentence, Logan comes tearing into the clearing. Running at breakneck speed, he leaps through the air and lands on top of Stone with a hard thud, his four paws digging into flesh and pinning his opponent to the ground.

Without missing a beat, Stone drives his fist into Logan's throat. Logan lets out a deep guttural sound then lunges for Stone's neck. But Stone gains the advantage over the other wolf, using that moment of distraction to roll out from underneath him. In two seconds flat, Stone tears his clothes from his body and shifts.

From my aerial position I watch them. Alpha pitted against alpha. They begin circling each other, both sizing up the enemy and looking for a weakness in the other that might give an advantage. When frothing mouths and deadly incisors flash beneath the overhead moon, I realize that only one wolf is going to walk away from here with me tonight.

Blood rushes through my veins and I struggle harder, determined to break myself free. If I don't stop the fight, I might never know what Stone is keeping from me.

Pain races up my leg, the wire digging tighter as I swing myself toward the tree. Nausea wells up inside me but I ignore it. I push harder and grasp the tree trunk, but only manage to tear my nails clear from my fingertips as I try to hang on.

Panicked, I watch the wolves fight each other, a tumbling mess of fur and claws as they roll around on the hard ground.

Logan gains purchase and begins mauling Stone. The sound of cartilage popping and bones crunching echoes in the dark. Frothy saliva drips from Logan's mouth and as his fangs slice through flesh, ripping skin from body, the fresh scent of blood fans out in the night. Yelping sounds reach my ears, and I know I have to do something.

I begin to call on my wolf, but the second I do, gunshots ring out in the night. Hunters!

Survival instincts kicking in, the wolves separate, and Logan moves toward me in a protective manner. Stone's glance goes from Logan, to me, and when he penetrates my barriers and briefly touches my mind I get the strangest sense that he hadn't come here to harm me.

He tears his glance away and stares at Logan. A moment of uncertainty dances in his pewter eyes, then he glances at the sharp blade on the ground beneath me.

Logan places his paw over it and snarls. As his growl mingles with the approaching voices, Stone takes off and all I see is the swish of his tail as he darts into the forest.

Logan shifts back to human and grabs the knife. Within seconds he slices through the wire to release the trap. I drop but he catches me before I hit the ground.

He deposits me in front of him and looks me over quickly. "We need to get out of here. Can you run?"

I nod and when I hear hunters closing in, I understand how much danger I've put us in. I work to disassociate myself from the pain in my ankle as we dart into the woods. Logan races to his pile of clothes, pulls them on and we run long and hard until we reach our campsite.

Logan points to the tent. "Go shift and heal your leg." He grabs one of the backpacks and starts filling it with supplies.

With a sense of urgency racing through me, I peer into the dark and lower my voice wanting to explain, to apologize. "Logan—"

He stops me with a firm shake of his head and I realize that he has every right to be angry with me. "Not right now, Pride," he says, and that's when I realize it's not anger I'm sensing. It's disappointment. "Just go."

As the sharpness in his voice cuts me, I slip into the tent and remove my clothes. I call on my wolf to mend my wounds and once I'm healed, I pull my clothes back on and step outside to find Logan waiting for me. He breaks down the small tent and attaches it to the pack.

Once finished, we sneak away, and lose ourselves in the

woods. We run long and hard until we're unable to run any longer. It's only after we've put a great deal of distance between us and the hunters that Logan drops the pack.

Both lost in our own thoughts, we remain silent as we set up the small tent. Once complete, we climb in and collapse under the stress of the night.

A few hours later, after a very fitful sleep, my lids spring open. I can hear birds chirping and I'm grateful that early morning is upon me. Logan stirs beside me, his body brushing mine. My pulse pounds hard in my neck when I think about how much danger I put him in last night. I also think that if it hadn't been for him, I could very well be on my way back to the compound, or worse, dead.

I think about my father's scent, think about how I reacted without thinking. I press the heels of my hands to my eyes and shake my head.

If there is one thing I've learned these past seventeen years it's that I need to think with my head not my heart. The latter will only end up getting me killed.

I remain quiet and think more about my father. Who set that trap with his scent? Stone? The PTF? Trackers? But more importantly, the master killed him years ago, so how did they have material with his scent on it?

Unless...

No. I have to be wrong. The master killed him. He told us so. Then again it's not like I can believe anything he says. My stomach clenches at the direction of my thoughts, and I force myself to think of something else. My father can't be alive. He just can't be. Because if he was, wouldn't he have tried to free me?

Not wanting to think about that any longer, my thoughts drift to Logan as I let him sleep a little longer. So much has changed over a few short days, yet I still know so very little about him. What is it about him that has my master so enraged? Is it simply because he is a tracker who broke free, or is it something else? My mind races with all the questions I still want to ask. It also races with the questions I want to ask Stone.

His soft whisper startles me. "You're awake."

It's a statement not a question.

"You are, too," I say lowering my voice to match his.

"What are you thinking about?"

"You."

The blankets rustle and his scent fills the tent as he leans toward me. He looks sleepy and rumpled and when his brow knits together with genuine worry, I pull my blankets tighter around me.

He touches my arm. "What happened to you last night, Pride? Why did you run away from me?"

"I caught my father's scent."

"But I thought you said your father——"

"I know. It was a trap. I reacted with my heart, not my head. It was stupid of me."

"It wasn't stupid," he says softly. "Sometimes we need to fight with our hearts. It can give us an edge."

I look at him and wonder if he's speaking from experience. But last night he fought with his intellect, not his heart, right?

I smooth my mussed hair off my face and think about his abilities. "If it wasn't for you and your skills..." I let my words fall off, hating to think what could have happened if he hadn't showed up.

His grins and I can tell he's trying to lighten my mood when he says, "It's all in the name."

I angle my head, needing to know more about him, needing to know more about this boy who understands so much. I think back to our initial meeting. "Exactly how you were able to remove the microchip?"

"In my old life I went to school. I learned a thing or two."

I stare at him. "You went to school?" My pulse leaps a bit and I can't help but feel envious of this boy who knows what it's like to lead a normal life. Well, as normal as can be for a wolf.

He grimaces. "Don't look so impressed. It's not all it's cracked up to be."

I go silent for a while and try not to think about the ache in my joints. But as the moon beckons me—one more day until it's full—I think about the campers, how nice they all were to us and how I could never live with myself if anything happened to them.

Drawn by a force I can't identify, I slide closer to Logan, and in a protective move he wraps his arm around me and pulls me close. As I lay there packaged in his strong arms, I suddenly feel like I'm on a roller coaster ride. My muscles tense and I force myself to relax.

He inches back. "Pride?" he asks quietly as his eyes search my face.

I blink rapidly. "Yes."

He looks me over. "What else is going on inside that head of yours?"

When I don't readily answer, he props his elbow up and rests his head in his hand. "Tell me."

After a long pause I finally say, "The full moon."

"What about it?"

I lower my eyes. "I can't control her." I turn to him and press my hand over my stomach. "Can you control your wolf?"

He nods.

I look away and think about the friends we made. "What if she—"

"She won't."

"How do you know?"

"Because you're with me now, Pride," he says, as if laying claim to me, marking me as his. "And I won't let anything happen to you. I promised you that already and I don't break my promises."

I swallow. "I'm not sure you can make that promise."

"You're going to have to trust me then, aren't you?"

I stare at him long and hard and while I know I feel something for this wolf, something I've never felt for another, old habits and lifelong fears die hard and I still can't forget about the secrets I know he's keeping from me.

"You can't ask me to do that."

His face hardens. "After everything we've been through, I think I can." But he doesn't press. Instead his fingers span my stomach. "First things first, we need to make sure your stomach is full."

"Okay."

"Are you ready to go hunting again?"

Feeling emotionally battered after my encounter with Stone, I push the blankets off me. I crouch on the balls of my feet and unzip the tent, needing to run and clear my head. Maybe a good hard trek through the woods will help me figure out what's going on.

"Let's go."

We sniff the air and look for game. As we track along the mountain, Logan moves ahead of me, to keep an eye out for danger and traps. As he leads the way, the sight of him pulls all my attention and I decide it's well past time to learn more about the boy who has yet to turn on me.

"Logan?"

"Yeah?" He slows until I'm beside him.

"How did my master find you?"

Pewter flickers in his eyes as they meet mine. "I don't know."

"Where was your master's estate?"

"California."

I wave my hand. "Then you must have been running for days if you made it here."

"I hitchhiked."

"When did you remove your microchip?"

"As soon as I escaped."

"Then how did they track you here?"

"Like I said, I don't know."

I glare at him and my stomach twists. He's asked me to trust him but once again I get the sense he's keeping something from me. I open my mouth to voice those concerns but he silences me and gestures with a nod.

When I see a pack of deer, I understand his intent and instantly begin to remove my clothes. It's only after I'm naked that I realize I hadn't turned my back on the alpha while I undressed. Once complete, I stand next to Logan like we're equals and we both call on our primal side.

A few minutes later, when we're both in wolf form, we silently communicate a plan of attack and begin our hunt. I calm my wolf and mentally go over yesterday's training as Logan gives me the go ahead.

I sniff the air and dart through the woods, keeping low and quiet, the way he taught me. As I approach I get a quick flash of panic, but then I hear Logan. He's in my head, working with me, coaching me and giving me the courage I need to make the kill.

*"That's it, Pride, you've got this."*

Strangely enough, there is something so encouraging in his voice, and the combination of his strength and belief in me help me push forward. Confidence bolstered, and wanting to please Logan, I dart forward, and catch the deer from behind. Within seconds I wrestle it to the ground and once it's down, Logan joins me. I can feel his excitement, his pride in me and my own chest swells in response.

We eat together and once we're done we go find our clothes and make our way to the lake for water.

Logan grabs two big sticks as we cut through the trees and once we reach the lake he sits on the embankment, pulls the knife from the bag and begins to shape the ends into a sharp spear.

"What's that for?" I ask as I take a big swallow of water.

"Fishing."

Even though I've just had breakfast, I can't deny that I'm ready for lunch. "You're a guy of many skills."

Logan smiles and peels a strip of bark off the stick. When the blade of the knife glistens in the sunlight it reminds me of Stone.

"Logan?" I begin.

"Yeah?"

As though sensing my unease Logan puts the knife down and shoots a glance around to do a quick check for danger.

"What is it?" he asks.

"Stone was trying to tell me something."

His face darkens at the mention of Stone. "What do you think it was?"

"I'm not sure, but I don't think he wanted to hurt me."

"That's not how it looked to me. He was coming at you with a knife." Logan holds up the metal blade and his voice is hard when he says, "This knife."

I steal a quick glance at him. "That's because you couldn't hear what he was saying to me."

"What are you talking about?"

"Stone and I, well, we can speak telepathically."

He gives me an odd look. "All wolves can, Pride."

"Not when they are in human form." As soon as the words leave my mouth, I feel like I've betrayed him somehow.

His body stiffen and when his eyes turn cold, I get the sense he knows something I don't.

"What?" I ask.

Logan goes quiet for a long moment, then he asks, "When did your master break Stone?"

"Three years ago when he turned sixteen."

His gaze shifts to my body. "And you were what, fourteen, going through puberty?"

"Yes."

"And this is right around the time he started acting aggressive around you right?"

"Yeah."

Logan scrubs his chin with his hand, briefly closes his eyes and makes a tortured sound. "I should have known."

"What?"

"Stone isn't your enemy, Pride." He gives a solemn shake of his head. "He's in love with you."

I balk at that suggestion. "You have no idea what you're talking about."

"Think about it. I'm sure your master was like mine and would use anything you loved or cared about against you right?"

My stomach cramps as I think about the elders and what the master will do to them because of me. "Yes."

"Maybe that's why Stone kept his feelings a secret and went so far as to let everyone believe he hated you."

Logan goes quiet for a minute to let me chew on that, but the idea is so farfetched I have a hard time working my mind around it.

His gaze lingers on my face for a long time. "That's what I would have done." His eyes narrow and his voice drops to a soft whisper when he adds, "If it meant protecting you, that's exactly what I would have done."

My mind spins as I take a moment to entertain the idea. "You're wrong."

"Just think about it," Logan says.

My brain comes to a screeching halt and I refuse to dwell on Logan's absurd suggestion, because I can't believe Stone is in love with me.

I command myself to get my thoughts together. "Maybe this is all ridiculous and Stone is nothing more than an aggressive alpha who always takes what he wants." I nod toward the knife. "And maybe he really was going to hurt me."

"Yeah, maybe," Logan says, sounding unconvinced.

"Come on, let's move."

"Don't you want to go fishing?"

I pull in a fortifying breath. "Maybe later," I say, needing to run, to hunt, to work off the nervous feeling churning in my gut.

Logan repacks the bag and hands me a spear. I take it and start running through the woods without bothering to push branches out of my way. I feel the sting of a thorn as it slices my face but I ignore the pain. As if sensing my turmoil Logan remains silent and lets me run hard as I work things through.

I run for a long time with Logan keeping a fair distance behind but then suddenly I get the strangest sense we're being followed. As my nape tingles in warning, the way it always does when danger is nearby, I slow my steps and glance around the rough terrain, noting how high up the mountain-top we are.

I spin around and look at Logan, who is staring back at me, but what I see has my senses going on high alert. My wolf growls and my buttons pop as my primal side threatens to make its presence known but my intuition tells me that my best bet at survival is to keep my human form.

I suck in a sharp breath and with my spear aimed directly at Logan's head, I say in a calm voice that belies my emotions. "Get on your knees, Logan."

Logan holds his hands up, palms out. "Pride," he whispers, and cocks his head to the side. "What are you doing?"

"Do it," I demand.

Expression troubled, he drops, and as I watch him my heart trip hammers.

With speed and accurate precision I throw the home-made spear at the mountain lion tracking us from behind. The sharp end skims its gorgeous coat, slicking along its fur just enough to maim it but not enough to kill it. Its loud roar echoes off the mountain-top, but the attack is enough to send it running in the opposite direction.

Logan swivels around and then his eyes dart back to mine. His grin comes slow. "Nice."

Hands shaking, I stand there trying to breathe. Then something very important occurs to me. In the heat of the moment I was thinking with my heart, not my head.

It also occurs to me that I've never been so fast, or so accurate before. But the thought of losing Logan gave me an adrenaline rush like I've never felt before. It was that adrenaline and the fight-or-flight response that came with it that helped me perform better.

Maybe Logan was right and fighting with your heart doesn't always have to be your downfall. Maybe, just maybe if you're fighting for something or someone you really care about it gives you an edge. I always sensed Stone was fighting with his heart, not his head. Had he been protecting me all this time? Is that why I'm still alive today? Could Logan have been right?

Logan's eyes narrow. "You okay?"

I begin to shake as I come down from the rush. Logan grabs me and hauls me against him and I see a flash of possessiveness in his eyes when he says, "Hey." Tenderness steals over him and he presses his lips to my temple.

"I'm okay," I say, comforted by his touch as his warmth moves through me, although if what he suspects about Stone is true then I don't believe I'm ever going to be okay again.

He makes a noise with his tongue and arches a brow. "You're lightning fast, Pride. When you come up against someone twice your size, they're really going to underestimate you."

I know what he's doing and because I'm such a trembling mess I let him do it.

"That's a nice advantage you have there," he continues. "Now I know why your master sent you after me."

A smile touches my mouth as Logan's little pep talk starts to make me feel better. I sniff, pull myself together, and give him a coy smile. "I believe I had you worried for a minute there, didn't I?"

He jabs his thumb into his chest, exaggerating when he says, "Me? No way."

I give him a dubious look and plant my hands on my hips. "Not even for a minute?"

"Okay." He forces a quick laugh. "Maybe for a minute. I guess I should be thanking you, young grasshopper."

I have no idea why he's calling me a grasshopper, but once again the oddest sense of pride wells up in my chest.

"No need to thank me," I say as I recall all the times he saved me. "Let's call it even."

He grins. "I've taught you well."

"Maybe you do need me after all." I toss the words over my shoulder as I move past him to collect my spear.

He slips an arm around my waist and spins me around until I'm facing him. He dips his head and when his hair falls forward, the scent of his skin washes over me. My entire body stirs to life.

Rich pewter flecks sparkle in his blue eyes and there is no humor in his voice when he says, "I never said I didn't need you, Pride."

As I look up at him, I wonder exactly when it was that I developed feelings for him and exactly when it was that we stopped acting like enemies and started working together. Then I quickly remind myself that we have no future. In a few short days, when we escape this place, I'll be leaving him behind, never to set eyes on him again.

"You're right," I answer, working diligently to harden myself. "You didn't."

He lets me go and I gather my spear, but when I turn back to Logan and see the bloodlust in his eyes my heart races. My hand goes to my throat, to where a thorny bush cut into my skin, and I feel the sticky drops of warm blood beneath my fingers.

"Logan?"

With two long strikes he closes the distance between us, and my wolf feels no fear as his glance settles on my throat. She only feels puzzled.

"What is it about my blood that makes you hungry?" I finally manage to get out.

He gives a frustrated shake of his head. "It's not hunger, Pride."

"Then what is it?"

He laughs and looks at me like I'm dense. "For a smart wolf you can be pretty naïve about certain things."

With that he turns and stomps ahead of me. Before he gets too far in front of me he says, "I need you to morph and heal yourself right now, before I do something I might regret."

A*ugust 28th one day until full moon*

**W**hile we work to avoid hunters we spend the daytime hours honing my skills as we make our way out of the park. Logan takes me higher and higher on the tallest mountain, to an area of the park that is off limits to hikers. I know why he's doing it, but still don't think the distance will prevent my untamed wolf from going after what she wants. When her bloodlust takes hold, anything can happen. I shiver at the thought and push down a burst of panic.

As daylight begins to recede and the moon rides across the dark sky I try to fight down an ominous sense of foreboding. I glance around and wonder what's keeping Logan. He left to gather snow to melt for coffee but seems to be taking an awfully long time.

Working to pass the time, I pace around the small camp-fire, feeling restless, edgy and so antsy it's all I can do to keep from shifting and sprinting full speed across the mountain-top.

"Easy, Pride," Logan says as he comes up behind me. He pulls me to him and my back presses against his chest. A rush of heat chases the chill away as he puts his mouth near my ear and says, "It's going to be okay."

I nod, even though I don't believe him. How can it possibly be okay? I'm an undisciplined wolf who is trained to kill and not even Logan will be safe when the moon reaches its peak.

He spins me around and those rich, intense eyes of his lock on mine. As I watch him wet his lips, tension coils through me, and I find it most difficult to think with any sort of clarity. This boy really does have the uncanny ability to throw me off my game.

"I know something that will take your mind off the shift," he murmurs with quiet certainty.

His voice is so soft, so suggestive and so loaded with promise my entire body quivers, and I wonder if he's going to kiss me.

I search his face. "What?" I ask, trying to keep my tone casual, my body from pulsing.

He grabs my hand, picks up our backpack and takes me to a soft spot on the hill. We plunk down on the grassy slope and he reaches into his bag. He pulls out a pen and paper and hands them to me.

"Why don't you draw something?"

I stare at him, completely unprepared for the emotions this gesture brings out in me.

I stumble over my words and ask, "How? Where?"

His dark brow shoots up, like he's surprised by the question. "You're always poking around in the sand with a stick, so I grabbed those back at the campfire."

His observations take me by surprise, even though I

realize they shouldn't, and pull me up short. I stare at him, dumbfounded.

"You might want to close your mouth, Pride. The flies are out tonight." With that he laughs quietly and sprawls out on the ground. He spreads his arms and legs wide and as he breathes deep he stares at the mosaic of stars overhead.

When his lids slip shut, I continue to stare at him long and hard, then turn my attention to the paper and begin to sketch. We don't speak, not for a long time, then I finally break the quiet.

"Someday I'd like to try painting." I'm not sure what compelled me to reveal that private detail about myself. Perhaps the planets have aligned themselves just right or perhaps I really want to share something personal with Logan.

His voice is soft and his eyes are still closed when he says, "Painting can be cool."

This surprises me. "You've painted?"

He opens one eye and peeks at me. "Sure. In art class."

We go quiet again for a moment and then he props himself up on his elbow. "Why do you always draw the ocean?"

I shrug. "There is something about the ocean that reminds me of freedom."

"Someday we're going to go there then," he says matter-of-factly as he plops back down.

I swallow hard and while I appreciate his offer, and as much as I'd like to hold out hope that someday we could actually go to the beach, I don't. In a few short days, once we clear the woods, lose the hunters, and make it past the full moon unscathed, I'll be gone from his life forever.

As I glance at the boy spread out on the ground beside me I can't deny that I've enjoyed his companionship and appreciate all he's taught me over the last few days, but I also can't deny that he's becoming something more to me than I should have allowed.

Logan rolls onto his side and his voice turns serious. "About tomorrow night."

"What about it?" I ask.

He moves closer. "You're going to have to listen to me. To do exactly what I say."

My hand stills over my paper and as his touch seeps into my skin it elicits a shiver from deep within.

"I can't guarantee it," I answer honestly. "I wish I could but I can't."

A growl rips from his lungs and pewter flares in his eyes. "If we're going to make it through this, I need you to listen to me."

As I feel his tension, my blood pounds hard and I glare at him, wondering exactly what it is he's planning. My mind shifts through all the situations he might think it's going to take to keep my wolf from attacking.

"I'll try."

"You're going to have to do better than that."

My stomach quivers. "Okay, then yes," I say, only because that's what he wants to hear, not because I believe it. Deep down I don't know if I can do what he asks of me.

He rolls onto his back. "Good." He goes quiet for a moment then takes me by surprise when he asks, "Are there any other wolves you can communicate with in human form?"

"No," I answer.

Darkness moves over his face. "Why do you think you have that connection with Stone?"

"I don't know." I look at him carefully, and there is something in his expression that has the hairs on my nape tingling. "Do you?"

Instead of answering he asks, "You both grew up in the compound together?"

"Yes."

"And he wants you to be his mate?"

"Yes."

"And you never wanted to be his?"

"No. He was cruel and aggressive."

Before I can ask him what he's getting at a twig crunches in the distance and we both still. Logan looks at me, a silent exchange as we both take a second to assess the danger. Logan goes up on his feet and crouches low, bracing his hands on the ground as he sniffs the cool air. I drop my pen and paper and pull the forest into my lungs, but when I catch a very familiar scent, one that has my hackles rising, my heart goes to my throat.

Stone!

I jump to my feet and spin around, trying to pinpoint his location. I know I should be afraid that he's tracking us, and I know I should probably flee, but my instincts dictate that I go on the offense, not the defense, and run after him. I need to get to the bottom of matters with him once and for all.

As I prepare for a face off, my canines push through my gums. I begin to walk toward his scent but Logan grabs my arm to stop me.

"I'll go."

"No. This is my fight."

His expression changes, darkens, and I can tell by the look he's aiming my way that he's not about to let me out of his sight. His turbulent gaze brushes over the menacing forest then turns back to me.

"What if I'm wrong, Pride? What if he wasn't protecting you?"

"What if you're not? What if he can help us?"

"What if it's a trap?"

"I have to know."

I pull away from him and dash into the woods, but Logan

is right on my tail and following close behind me. I sniff the foliage until I come to a spot where Stone's scent is the strongest. I stop, spin around, and peer into the darkness, but Stone is nowhere to be found.

"He was here." I point to my feet. "He was right here." I try to calm myself because my voice is bordering on hysteria and under the circumstances I can't afford to let my emotions get the better of me. I shuffle around, confused. "He was watching us."

"And now he's gone."

A shiver runs through me to think Stone had been so close, watching. Listening. So why didn't he attack?

"What could that mean?" I ask.

Logan's look is dark, piercing. Deadly. "One of two things, I guess. He either felt outnumbered and left to get help, or he's letting you go."

I try to wrap my brain around those two possibilities. "The Stone I know would never let me go." I think of the dress, his years of aggression toward me, and Logan's theory behind Stone's actions. Is it possible that I could have been so wrong about him?

"Then if he shows up again, I'll kill him."

I swallow at the calmness I hear in Logan's voice and it simply reminds me that he's a dangerous alpha, a skilled hunter. A predator, who, when threatened, would kill in seconds flat, without an ounce of hesitation.

"Either way, we can't stay here," he says.

"It doesn't matter where I go, he'll track me by scent."

"Then we'll keep moving, and stay one step ahead of him."

I nod, and because I've never trusted Stone, and decide I'm not about to now, I think it's a good plan.

With that we pack our bag, hastily shoving our supplies into the various compartments before we take off on foot. We can cover more ground if we travel on all fours, but we don't want to leave our supplies behind. That, and the PTF will most likely be looking for two wolves.

As we push through the thick foliage and lose ourselves in the night the moon filters through the heavy leaves overhead. My joints ache like mad and it reminds me that come tomorrow night, I'll no longer be the only undisciplined wolf out here, running free for the first time on shift night.

Will the handlers reel Stone in before he morphs, or will they send him after me when his wolf is at its strongest? Even if Stone isn't out to harm me—and the jury is still out on that —will his bloodlust take over or will his wolf have what it takes to back away a second time?

*August 29th night of full moon*

When the sun begins its early morning ascent, Logan and I stop running and collapse beneath a towering oak tree. As I steal a glance around to assess the area for signs of danger, I feel like a taut bow ready to snap at any second. Every muscle in my body is tight and as the waxing moon pulls harder and harder at my wolf, I can feel my patience wearing thin.

"Let's get a drink and go hunting," Logan suggests when he sees the troubled state I'm in.

I nod, and wipe the moisture from my forehead, but know hunting is only a temporary distraction. At the end of the day, it's going to take a lot more than a simple diversion like hunting to keep me from going against my nature.

We spend the day stalking prey, running and working hard to fill our stomachs. As we fully exhaust our bodies I wonder if this is all Logan has up his sleeve. If so, then I believe we're going to be in a heap of trouble.

When I tire of his tactics I decide to draw, but can't seem to keep my concentration for any length of time. Restless and edgy, I toss the pen and paper aside, and track along the edge of the snow-packed summit.

The hours slowly slip by and throughout the long day Logan doesn't trail too far from me, and I note the way he keeps me under his watchful eye.

I pace impatiently as he assembles the tent deep in the thick of trees, hidden from view, and can feel the worry in his gaze when he looks at me. And I can't help but think he should be worried. Not only for those hikers, but for himself.

Looking for a distraction, I climb to the peak of the mountain and stare at the rough terrain still ahead of us. My breath turns to fog in front of my face as my eyes search the landscape. Not too far off in the distance I can see a hint of civilization. As I zero in on the buildings, my pulse leaps with hope, understanding we've almost made it to the other side of the park.

Tomorrow if we rise early and hit the trails, I'm sure we can reach the Canadian border before dark. We're so close I can almost taste the freedom. But then another thought strikes. A darker one. Does Logan have what it takes to tame me so we can both make it out of here alive?

I guess I won't know that answer until tonight, when we're both under the power of the full moon.

I pull my coat tighter around me to ward off a chill as I jump from the peak and watch Logan walk around our makeshift camp. As he moves like a predator, with one eye on me at all times my heart misses a beat.

We've grown close over the last few days, closer than I should have allowed, and I really don't want to turn on him. I also can't risk him turning on me. After all, at our core we're animals ruled by instinct and survival of the fittest. Then again after everything we've been through, my gut tells me this boy would never do anything to harm me.

I wish I could say the same about myself.

I bite down on the inside of my cheek hard enough to draw blood. Maybe I should go, run, flee the safe haven of his arms and get as far away from him as possible. And I can't forget about Stone. I dart a nervous glance around the woods. If he's out here stalking me, aren't I simply putting Logan in more danger by staying close?

"Don't even think about it."

I spin around and gasp when I find Logan invading my personal space. His overwhelming presence throws me off balance and practically steals the air from my lungs.

"What are you talking about?" I question.

"You're not going anywhere, so don't even try."

My joints take that moment to ache and when the moon pulls harder, awakening my hunger, I realize how dire the situation is.

"How did you know?"

"I might not be Stone but that doesn't mean I don't know what you're thinking."

There is something in his voice when he says Stone's name. Something that makes me think he's envious of my ability to communicate with Stone.

"You're not safe with me around," I say.

"I'll take my chances."

"What if I—"

He offers me a reassuring smile and it doesn't only mess with my body, it messes with my brain. "You won't. I can help you, little one."

Having grown fond of his nickname for me, I can't help but smile. "You're pretty sure of yourself."

He drags me to him and his face softens when he presses his lips to my forehead. "I'm also sure of you."

"Don't be," I say and note the sudden urgency in my voice, one I've never heard before. Frustrated, I lightly pound on his chest and add, "Unless you have some tricks up your sleeve that I don't know about."

He rolls one broad shoulder and I note a hint of nervousness in his voice when he says, "Maybe I do."

As I watch him, I realize I've only heard uncertainty in his voice one time before, and that was when we were alone in the tent. "I sure hope so."

He grips my arms and inches me back. The warmth in his eyes ignites a fire in my stomach when he says, "Make sure you concentrate on my voice only, okay?"

I open my mouth to speak, but slam it shut again when I hear a noise in the underbrush. Logan and I turn to catch sight of a rabbit as it darts past our tent.

When my wolf yelps, wanting to be unleashed, to take chase at the first warm-blooded thing she sees, I know in a few short hours we're all going to be in serious trouble.

I step away from Logan and continue to pace. When I come across the backpack I root around inside and find the last of our provisions. A cinnamon-coated granola bar. I tear it open and split it in half. I hand Logan his share and chew slowly on mine as I once again lose myself in my own thoughts.

As the daylight disappears and douses the woods in darkness, I can feel the full moon taunting me.

I shy away from it and stare at the snow-dusted ground beneath my feet, trying to focus on anything and everything except that old familiar call of the wild and what it's about to do to me.

At the glacier-capped peak of the mountain, ice shards crunch beneath my boots, the sound cutting through the silence of the night. I peer over the jagged cliff and my glance instantly darts to some campers hiking through the lush green valley some eight hundred feet below.

Deep inside my wolf stirs, letting me know what she wants. What she's been trained to do. The hairs on the back of my neck prickle and a shiver moves through me. I carefully back away from the embankment, away from temptation.

My eyes slip shut as I diligently fight an internal battle to defy nature. I realize it's impossible, but it still doesn't stop me from trying to resist the power the moon has over my kind.

When a rough, callused palm touches my cheek, the gentle caress a clear attempt to settle my unease, my lids spring open, and I suck in a sharp breath.

"It's okay, Pride. I'm here."

The softness in Logan's voice draws me in and trickles down my spine like warm summer rain. I can feel him—too close. I try to inch away, but he doesn't let me. He grips my arms and pulls me to him. When our bodies collide, my head jerks up with a start and my gaze clashes with his. The silver glow from the full moon highlights the pewter in his eyes and just below the surface I can see his wolf pacing.

Strong fingers rake through my long, tangled hair and draw my head against his chest. He dips his chin and buries his face in my knotted curls. With the softest voice, he murmurs, "You have to trust me."

Trust?

I eye him with uncertainty. After everything we've been through, I want to trust him, but I know what my wolf wants.

What she's capable of.

I shake my head and struggle to pull away, but he grasps me tight and splays one large palm over the small of my back, his warm, powerful hand attempting to chase away my unease.

"I can get you through this," he assures me. A gentle tug on my hair forces me to look at him. "I promise I won't let you hurt anyone."

His soothing words do little to calm me. Not when I know what my wolf is capable of.

"What if you can't? What if I—"

"You won't." He pulls me in tighter to offer reassurance and presses his mouth against my temple. His soft lips brush over my skin and in a moment of weakness I accept his warmth, my wolf taking comfort in his quiet strength and allowing it to help me forget what I am and the danger I pose to those innocent people below.

Logan makes a strange noise, a half-laugh, half-growl and dips his head. With our lips only inches apart, his hair brushes over my cheek and he pulls me closer, anchoring me to him. As he packages me in his arms, my throat constricts and heat explodes inside me.

"Logan," I begin and wet my lips. When I see turbulence in his eyes, I wonder if he's going to pull away from me again, or is this the moment when he's finally going to kiss me.

"Yes?"

Before I can answer his lips find mine and I gasp as a shiver wracks my body. But Logan doesn't pull back, doesn't address my shock. Instead, as foreign sensations explode inside me, he deepens the kiss and takes full possession of my mouth.

When he growls, need unfurls inside me and a fine shudder licks up my spine, catching me off guard. As intense pleasure courses through my veins, it instantly distracts me from the temptation below. For a moment I forget about those campers, the full moon, and the hunger gnawing in my stomach. I concentrate only on the sensations slamming into me as I let them pull me under like a tsunami wave. Never in my life have I felt such heat in my blood, such excitement bubbling up inside me.

His hands settle on my hips and when he draws me closer, I can't seem to think with any clarity. When his fingers bite into my skin hard enough to leave a bruise, I begin to unravel like an old woolen scarf.

His heat reaches out to me and a split second later my world tilts on its axis. Feeling dizzy, I focus on the sweet cinnamon flavor of his mouth, knowing I'm about to melt like a summertime Popsicle. Good God, I've never been kissed like this before.

Never like this.

"Kiss me back, Pride," he murmurs into my mouth. I part my lips and as his scent swirls around me sweat breaks out on my body.

Caught up in the moment I let myself get lost in his touch. His hands slide to my back and he holds me tighter. Despite the urgency of the situation, he doesn't rush things. Instead, we exchange kisses for a long time, until heat spreads through my entire body and my blood fires from simmer to inferno.

A raging fever builds inside me, but this time it's not from his touch, or from the brush of his lips over mine. Powerless to resist the pull of the moon, I break free from his hold and step back. Logan's silver eyes rake over me and it's all I can do to catch my breath as my primal side wrestles for dominance.

My clothes rip and I realize that I've left no time to remove them. But I can't think about such things right now, not with the way my wolf is clawing its way out of my body. As always, blinding pain sears my insides and I clutch my stomach. Heat boils my blood and I arch my back and let loose a deep, guttural moan.

"Stay with me, Pride. Listen to my voice."

My legs wobble and I drop to the ground next to my

shredded clothes. The groaning of my joints, sliding and shifting into place, cuts through the quiet around us. Tawny colored fur sprouts from my skin and shelters my exposed flesh from the harsh mountain elements.

Logan drops to the snow-packed ground beside me, waiting for me to complete my transformation before he begins his own. His age and strength make him much more adept at prolonging the change.

My muzzle punches out of my mouth, and the world around me begins to alter, fading in and out of existence. Blood pumps quickly through my veins and that's when I notice the hunger churning inside me. I turn away from Logan and savagely toss my head from side to side.

"Focus on me," Logan's deep voice commands.

My nails extend and with much effort I angle my chin to see him. Rainbows of color swirl before my eyes, and then the forest fades to a dull gray. I try to concentrate on his voice. But the pain is too much. Burning. Intense. I cry out.

As my cartilage slides into place, my girlish scream turns into a dark howl. It echoes off the mountain and sends a flock of birds into flight. Silence falls once more as I pull my lips back to expose sharp fangs.

A split second later, the last of my bones reform and as the pain begins to ebb, I gingerly sit back on my haunches and proceed to groom myself as I draw my next breath as a wolf.

Looking through the eyes of the beast, I glance around, fully aware of the boy studying my every movement. With my transformation complete, I watch him in return. Modesty aside, Logan sheds his clothes and his loud howl cuts the twilight as he joins me in primal form.

A few seconds later he stands before me as a beautiful boy trapped in a wolf's body—a lethal combination of power, muscle and intellect. The cool night wind ruffles the dark fur on his streamlined body as he circles me, coming dangerously close to my undisciplined wolf, and I wonder what he's going to do next.

His paws sink into the snow, each step tentative, careful. He'd been so confident before my shift, but now that he's staring at my wolf, wild and hungry beneath the full moon, I can see the caution in his eyes. Is he finally aware of what I'm capable of or is something else making him nervous?

A noise at the base of the mountain cracks the still air. Instincts sharpened, my ears perk up and I listen carefully. From my perch I can hear their voices, their laughter, and take joy in the sound of their blood rushing through their veins. It teases my hunger to the point of distraction. Driven by dark need, I canter to the cliff's edge and run my tongue over sharp canines.

*"Hey,"* Logan barks out.

I turn back to him.

*"I bet you can't catch me."* He twists around and with lightning speed bolts through the thick forest.

I scent the air and let loose a yelp, my wolf unable to resist the chase, the thrill of the hunt. Feeling feral, I dig my talon-like nails into the hard ground and with a swish of my tail I take off after him, following his distinct, earthy aroma, one I've grown quite fond of over the past few days. As I watch him weave his muscled body in and out of the tall, threadbare trees, I wonder where he's leading me. I also wonder what will happen when I catch him.

Will my instincts to kill rule my actions? Can I trust that his animal bloodlust won't take over?

Logan tosses me a glance over one powerful shoulder, and begins to slow to a trot. As I hurry to catch up, I note the way his dark gaze zeroes in on my throat which makes me wonder, does this boy have what it takes to tame me, or will tonight end in total and utter bloodshed for all?

When I stop a few feet away from him, pacing like the wild animal I am, anxious to kill, to feed, I look past his shoulder and notice the small crevice in the rock wall. Logan takes a cautious step backward and when he disappears into the cave, I let loose a deep, guttural howl. The low-pitched sound serrates the quiet night and sends the wildlife scurrying through the forest.

From the cavern I see a flash of pewter and it sends my wolf into chase. Untamed, I pounce inside the small opening. I look from the left to the right, but before I can locate Logan, his low growl punctures the black and he leaps through the air, pinning me belly up beneath him. My wolf howls and I push him off me. He rolls to the side and I climb on top of his powerful body determined to restrain him beneath my paws.

Logan, however, has other ideas. With ease, he flips me back over. He uses his power and strength to restrain me beneath him, and when I feel his sharp fangs cut into my throat, I let loose an agonized yelp.

He holds me down and as blood pours from my neck the smell saturates the tight quarters. As I feel the sting of his fangs, I know in an instant, it's kill or be killed.

I struggle beneath him, my paws thrashing, yet I'm still unable to gain purchase. With animal bloodlust ruling me, I fight, bite and scratch until I exhaust myself, but Logan still doesn't waver, still doesn't let go of my throat.

That's when it hits me. If he was going to snap my neck, wouldn't he have done it by now? I stop struggling.

"*Are you done?*" he asks fiercely.

Confused and breathing hard I don't answer. Instead I stare at him, and note the warm heat in his eyes as they lock on mine. That flash of heat does something to my wolf. Something primal. Something that settles my bloodlust.

"*Are you done, Pride?*" he asks again.

"*I thought you were going to—*" I answer, breathless.

"*I know what you thought.*"

"*It's…it's my wolf,*" I say apologetically. "*She doesn't know any better.*"

With that Logan eases back and releases his hold on me. I take that opportunity to flip onto my feet. Crouching low I watch him, watch the way his streamlined body flexes as he stalks toward the entrance. He uses his shoulder to roll a boulder in front of the small opening, locking himself inside with the dangerous wolf while keeping the rest of the world out.

"*What are you doing?*" I ask cautiously as my body heals the puncture marks on my throat.

"*Protecting you. Like I promised.*"

But when he turns back, and I see the hungry way he's looking at me, needy sensations erupt in my stomach and my caution turns to anticipation.

Because everything inside me tells me his hunger isn't for my blood.

Energy arcs between us as Logan stalks close. My entire body shivers, my wolf suddenly so completely aware of the alpha it's all I can do to draw in air.

Then it occurs to me. This is the distraction he's been planning. A female is programmed to seek an alpha, especially on shift night—a night when a male finds his mate. I don't miss the significance in what he's doing, what he's asking of me.

He circles me, keeping a wide berth. For a longtime neither of us speaks. We square off, a hush coming over us as time slips by, minute by minute, hour by hour, the moon outside riding higher in the sky, then slipping lower as it begins its descent. He finally breaks the quiet and says, "*You have to want this.*"

As I stare at him heat explodes through me and I know I

want this. I know I want Logan even though the idea of mating is foreign, exciting. Terrifying.

He stops moving, the wild glow in his eyes eliciting a shiver from deep within me. He stares at me for a long moment, and I can feel his tension like it's my own. My body calms as with the approach of twilight, and we both shift back, the moon no longer controlling us.

He holds his hand out to me and says, "Meet me half-way, Pride."

We exchange another long look, and the second I take a step toward him, he moves swiftly, closing the distance between us. As I absorb his warmth, I can hardly believe what we're about to do. How much I want to do this.

His hands seek mine and when he finds them trembling, he says, "I won't do anything to hurt you, Pride," he whispers.

"I know," I say as my stomach flutters.

And I do know.

He trails his fingers over my arm, and my skin comes alive as he touches me with soft hands. His muscles bunch, and I can feel heat coloring my cheeks as a shudder races through me. As I lose myself in the sensations, he slides an arm around me and pulls me close. I swallow, and can feel his heart pound erratically against his ribcage.

He brushes his thumb over my mouth, and I instinctively part my lips. A low growl rumbles in his throat as he dips his head and takes full possession, his tongue slipping inside to mate with mine. When I moan, he deepens the kiss, and I shake with an intensity that is both exhilarating and frightening.

"Touch me, Pride," he murmurs, his voice thinning to a whisper. "Please touch me."

I put my hands on his shoulders, and he sucks in a tight breath. I lightly trail my nails over his naked flesh, and raw desire sears my inside when I feel the strength of his muscles.

My hands skim his body, then tangle in his hair as I breathe in the scent of his skin and revel in the taste of his mouth.

I begin to shake all over, and when my knees buckle, Logan holds me tighter. He drops to the ground, pulling me with him, and that's when I notice the blanket.

He carefully lowers me onto it, and climbs over me. Everything in the way he's touching me, treating me like I could break at a moment's notice, makes me feel so beautiful, so special.

Intense eyes full of need meet mine as he pushes my hair from my face and my pulse leaps wildly.

"I want you so much," he murmurs. When I don't say anything, he looks at me. "Tell me you want me, Pride. Tell me you need this as much as I do."

"I want you," I somehow manage to get out around a tongue gone thick. "I need you, Logan."

His burning mouth comes down hard, claiming me, branding me with his heat. My stomach soars, heat flooding my veins. As his tongue plays with mine, I can feel the hardness between his legs. A strange strangled cry lodges in my throat.

He abandons my mouth and his lips scorch my skin as he slides lower, pressing hungry kisses to my chin, my neck, my shoulder.

His breath is coming harder now, and when his lips trail lower and find my hard nipple, a tremor rips through me.

"Logan," I cry out, my hands raking through his hair as it sweeps against my bare flesh.

My skin burns, and my body aches as his hands move over my body and when he reaches between my legs, awareness quivers through me.

He touches my inner thigh, stroking softly as he shifts his body weight to the side.

"Open your legs for me," he whispers, and I flush at the intimacy in his tone.

I inch my thighs open and when I hear his groan, feel his fingers touching my most private parts, desire twists inside me.

He strokes me gently, his touch creating a new intimacy between us.

His warm breath tickles my skin and my chest rises and falls as he caresses me, prepares me. His mouth goes to my stomach, and he kisses a path back up my body as his fingers slide deeper.

My hips lift, and I pinch my eyes shut as I welcome him into my body.

"Look at me," he says and when my lids open, I find Logan staring at me, pure desire in his eyes.

Small breasts crush against his chest as he pushes my hair from my face. "Are you ready for this?" he asks, his breath coming in ragged bursts as he settles himself on top of me.

Warmth spreads over my skin and I swallow, because I know nothing could have ever prepared me for this.

For Logan.

I nod, and as I begin to tremble from head to toe, he better positions himself. My hands slide over his back, and his heat scorches me as he pushes deep inside my body, joining us as one.

Pain slices through me and when a cry lodges in my throat he pulls out.

"I don't want to hurt you," he says, the tenderness in his voice turning me inside out. "Tell me to stop, and I will."

I touch his face. "I don't want you to stop." Pinned beneath him, I start moving, forcing him back inside me, and he grips my hair harder.

"Pride," he groans.

"Please," I say

With that he pounds into me, so hard and so fast it steals the breath from my lungs. We hold each other like our lives depend on it, and maybe on some level they do.

Logan buries him mouth in the hollow of my neck and as he pumps, I know he's seeking more than release.

A whimper escapes my lips as he stirs things inside, touching me in places so deep, a sense of belonging comes over me. Moisture breaks out on our flesh as we both give and take, making love as we ride out the last of the full moon.

Logan thrusts once, twice, then stills inside me. He throws his head back and I hold him tight as he legs go. After a moment he collapses on top of me. As his weight presses down on me, I lay there and bask in the glow of his touch, emotions raging inside me. He lifts his head to see me. "Did I hurt you?"

"No," I answer.

"You're not a very good liar," he says. "Next time will be better for you, Pride. I promise."

He rolls beside me and pulls me against him. As he gently runs his fingers up and down my arm, I try to shut down my emotions, not wanting to think about tomorrow or what it might bring.

We stay inside the cave until night bleeds into day and the first traces of light are upon us. When the full moon finally sleeps, we continue to touch, continue to acquaint ourselves with each other's bodies.

A long time later exhaustion pulls at us both and with our arms and legs in a tangled knot we fall into a deep slumber.

I have no idea how long I've been asleep but when I hear a noise at the mouth of the cave, I struggle to blink my eyes open. Caught somewhere between sleep and consciousness I try to focus, try to wipe the blur from my brain.

Unclear if I'm dreaming or not, I glance up to see a familiar figure standing over me. My pulse leaps. "*Stone!*"

I watch the way he's looking at me, the way he always looks at me. Dark eyes move over my bare body, then slide to naked boy sleeping beside me. Oddly enough when I realize what Stone sees—what he knows—I feel a strange sense of disloyalty.

Without speaking, he turns and makes a move to go.

"*Wait,*" I say and rush on. "*What's going on, Stone? What are you doing out here? What have you been trying to tell me?*" I know I'm rambling but can't seem to help myself. Rattled, I continue, "*Tell me please. Tell me about the number sequence. I don't understand.*"

He twists back around and as his glance falls over me, I can sense his struggle, feel a myriad of emotions tearing him up inside. Despite his turmoil, his words are slow and steady when he says, "*The master installed a new state of the art security system. I wanted you to know the code.*"

I blink, confused. "*Why?*"

"*To help you escape?*"

Escape? Stone wanted to help me escape?

"*I don't understand. How do you know the code?*"

"*You're not the only one who has been watching and listening.*"

I struggle to make sense of things. "*No one's been able to break out before, so why now, after all these years did he install a new security system?*"

"*I think the alarm system has more to do with keeping someone or something out, rather than keeping us in. It's like he's expecting an army to come for him.*" I hear a shudder in his breath and feel his anger when he says, "*One way or another I was going to get you out of there, Pride. Before anything happened to you.*"

My head spins and I sort through Stone's chaotic visions, trying to make sense of things, then suddenly the tumblers begin to slide into place. "*You were going to fight a handler?*"

At first surprise moves over his face, then he answers, "*Yes, on shift night.*"

*"The night we were supposed to mate."*

*"The night I was going to break you out."*

"No," I say shaking my head. *"You wanted to break me, not break me out."*

His tone softens. *"Don't you see? I needed the mating as a cover. It was the only way I could get the master to put us in a cell together."*

*"Stone,"* I choke out. *"The handler would have killed you."*

*"I would have fought,"* he whispers, then I hear a hitch in his voice when he adds, *"For you, I would have fought."* He takes a quick look at Logan and the sadness I see on his face rips though me like a silver bullet.

*"You would have died!"* I scream.

He doesn't respond, instead he says, *"You need to wake up, Pride. Now. You need to get moving."*

With apprehension surging inside me, I jolt upright in the cave and rub the sleep from my eyes. My gaze instantly darts to the spot where I'd seen Stone standing, but when my glance comes up empty my insides churn. I twist to see Logan, still sound asleep beside me and my mind races.

Had I simply dreamt it?

I shoot a glance around the cave and a barrage of emotions tear through me, unsure of what's happening.

Logan stirs awake beside me. His eyes open and he smiles when our gazes meet, but when he sees my distress, his smile dissolves and panic spreads across his face. He sits upright and reaches for me.

"Pride, what is it? Are you okay?"

"I'm okay," I lie, not at all certain I'll ever be okay again. "It was just a dream," I say, more to convince myself than anything else, because I can't bear to think that Stone was really here, that a wolf who I thought was my sworn enemy—a wolf who was planning to die for me—just had his heart torn out because I've given myself to another.

● 15

*August 30<sup>th</sup> waning moon*

**S**tark naked after a night in the cave with Logan, we make our way back to our tent. I gather my torn clothes and look them over. With a tuck here and fold there I figure I can still wear them.

As I dress I try not to think about Stone, try not to let the pain on his face haunt me.

Had he been here?

Or was it merely a dream?

Confused, I breathe deep to see if there are any lingering traces of his scent in the air, but when Logan's familiar aroma fills my nostrils, not Stone's, I shake my head to clear it, unable to make sense of it all.

Logan tosses the pack over his back and puts his arm around my waist, a gesture that fills me with warmth. "How do you feel?"

He looks so sleepy and rumpled that it has my mind racing to what we did in the cave. Then a grave thought hits me. Was it merely a diversion tactic on his part? Or does he really want me to be his mate?

"Last night, when we, you know, was it because—"

His grin is slow, soft and a smile reaches his eyes as he rakes my hair off my face. "It was because I wanted to, Pride. I've wanted to do that with you for a very long time now."

A surge of warmth floods me. "Then why didn't you? Why did you wait for so long?"

He gives a soft laugh. "Because whether you realized it or not you were vulnerable, and I wasn't going to take advantage of that. You needed to come to terms with your own feelings before you could come to terms with mine."

"So you have feelings for me then?" I ask, my voice rough with emotion.

His brow lifts in amused awareness then he laughs out loud. "For a smart girl—"

My heart tightens and I press my lips to his to stop him before he can finish. When I finally pull away surprise registers on his face.

He quirks a perplexed brow. "What was that for?"

I think about the last few days, think about where I would have been without him. My voice comes out a little shaky when I say, "I think you know."

All humor fades from his eye when he says, "And I think it's time for you to know, too."

Not liking the sound of that I tense and take a small step back. "Know what?" I ask cautiously, my entire body tightening at the seriousness I hear in his voice.

He lowers his tone, like he thinks it will help soften the blow when he says, "I'm not who you think I am."

In an instinctive move, my throat tightens and my nape prickles in warning. "What are you talking about?" I begin to move away, trying to wrap my head around this unexpected turn of events.

"Pride. Don't." Logan grabs my arms, but there is something in the way he says my name that immobilizes me.

"Who are you then?" I ask.

He goes quiet for a moment then says, "You remember when you asked if I believed there were packs who roam free in Canada? Compassionate wolves who live normal lives amongst the population and take to the woods on shift night?"

I watch him carefully, and give him a look that conveys my unease. "Yeah. Why?"

"Well they do exist. And that's where we're going."

Incredulous, my eyes widen. "You're telling me you know for a fact that they really do exist?"

"That's exactly what I'm telling you."

"How do you know?"

"Because I'm one of them."

He goes quiet and lets me look at him long and hard as I sort things through in my mind. My glance pans his face searching for the truth, but there is nothing in his expression or his body language to suggest he is lying to me.

I shake my head and realize I shouldn't be surprised at what I'm hearing. All the signs were there, waiting to be pieced together. As I think about his knowledge of the woods, his ability to hunt, to remove the microchip, to fit in so easily with the hikers, the puzzle known as Logan finally begins to fall into place.

Still, I remain cautious when I ask, "If you're telling the truth, why did you wait so long to tell me?"

"Would you have believed me?"

"I don't know."

"Well I do know and what I know is that you wouldn't have believed me for a minute. I've learned that trust isn't something that comes easy to you, Pride." There is a real sadness in his eyes when he lowers his head and I hear gentle understanding in his voice when he says, "After everything you've been through it's not much wonder. It took forever for you to trust me."

While I know he's right and that trust isn't something that comes easy to me, I still can't help but feel he betrayed me. "You still should have told me."

"Let me ask you something. If you thought I was trying to lead you somewhere would you have run in the opposite direction?"

"Yes," I say without hesitation. "I would have."

"That's why I didn't tell you. You're a girl to lead, not a girl to be led."

"Okay, fair enough." I incline my head, smooth down my ripped shirt and ask, "So you got captured, broke free, and now you're trying to find your way back home?"

He nods and runs his hands along the back of my neck. "I'm trying to get us both home."

My heart hitches. "You want to take me to your home?"

"Of course I do. I need you, Pride." He glances around. "I couldn't have made it this far without you."

"I wouldn't have made it without you, either."

As I mull things over longer and realize what this really means for me, a surge of excitement rushes through my veins. I take a moment to think more about his family in the Canadian mountains and give further consideration to the compassionate pack of wolves that live normal lives, wolves that work together, and only take to the woods on run night.

My heart races a little faster and a plan begins to formulate in my brain. My mother once thought this pack could help her, which was why she tried to make it across the border. Now that I know such a pack exists I begin to wonder if it's possible. Would they be willing to help me take down my master?

"If we can make good time today, we can be at the ferry by dinner time."

I'm already stepping over brush and pushing branches out of my way.

"We might have a small problem though."

I stop and my hair whips around my face when I turn back to him. "What?"

"You don't have a passport, and in order to get into Canada you're going to need one."

"Do you have one?"

"I have one stashed in the dash of my car. It's been in the parking lot at the ferry dock since my capture." He pulls a face and says, "Let's hope it's still there."

We're so close I refuse to give up now. "We need a plan."

"You'll have to shift to wolf."

My head comes up with a start. "You want me to shift? Won't the PTF be all over that place?"

"Probably a few trackers, too. But they'll be looking for two humans, or two wolves. They won't be looking for a guy with his dog."

"I'm not a dog. I'm a wolf," I remind him.

"Yes, but once again your size proves to be an advantage for us." I stare at him, still unconvinced. "You're small enough to pass yourself off as my pet, Pride."

He's right and I have to remember to start thinking of my size as a positive trait, not a negative one.

He pauses and asks, "So what do you think? Do you trust me enough to shift and put your fate in my hands?"

Without hesitation I say, "I put myself in your hands last night, didn't I?"

He smiles. "Good. Then let's do this."

Working side by side, we finish packing our supplies, and

take to the woods. We walk long and hard and I have a million questions for Logan, wanting to know more about his family as we make our way out of the forest. Would they be the kind to help? I've never asked anyone for help before and honestly wouldn't even know how to begin.

The time passes quickly as he fills me in on his life. The schools he's gone to, the houses he's lived in, and those he calls family. I learn that he lives on a quiet cul-de-sac with his aunt, uncle and his teenage cousin Gem who happens to be the same age as me.

I like listening to his stories and I can't help but feel a seed of hope blossoming inside me that maybe, just maybe if his pack can help me free the others we can all return to Canada and live normal lives.

After hiking for nearly five hours straight, we grab a drink from a bubbling brook and try to wash the grime from our faces before we reach civilization.

I help Logan smooth his hair down, and he wets his thumb and scrubs a streak of mud from my cheek.

He smiles at me. "My family is going to love you." Then his smile dissolves and I see a streak of jealousy when he adds, "So are all the alphas."

That makes me think of Stone and a lump lodges in my stomach. "I don't think—"

"I do," he says and cuts me off. "Come on."

Discussion closed he grabs my hand and we walk a few more hours until the Olympic Park is finally at our backs. As we exit, I glance around the small coastal town and catch sight of the ferry, which has just begun to unload vehicles at the dock. I also see two PTF officers patrolling the area and my stomach plummets.

When they turn in the opposite direction, Logan clasps my hand harder and we dart across the street. Without the cover of darkness to camouflage ourselves Logan pulls me between two towering buildings.

He glances over his shoulder and scans the street. Fortunately with the ferry in dock and everyone waiting to reload the town is bustling with activity. With any luck we can use the crowds to our advantage.

"Our best bet is to separate. You stay here and I'll go get the car. Once I get it, I'll pull up and block the alleyway. Use that time to shift and then jump into the passenger seat."

"Okay, got it."

Despite the urgency of the situation, he stops and places his hands on my arms. I watch his blue eyes darken and listen to his blood rush faster. His glance moves over my face. As he takes me in, like it's the last time he's going to see me, I suddenly get a horrible feeling in my gut.

He opens his mouth and I can tell he wants to say something. But when turbulent emotions pass over his eyes, he seems to change his mind.

"Be careful," he murmurs, then he drops a hard kiss onto my mouth and moments before he breaks free and disappears into the crowd I get a sinking sensation in the pit of my gut that he has just given me a goodbye kiss.

With danger all around me I need to stay sharp so I have no time to examine his actions, or how they make me feel. I draw a calming breath and crouch low, clearing my mind of everything, except the officers patrolling the dock. I scent the air, but with the dumpster so close behind me the smell of rotting compost and sewer clogs my senses.

Logan strolls through the streets, hiding in the wide open. I can't help but admire his confidence and skill as he makes his way to the parking lot near the dock, to where his car sits waiting.

I watch him carefully, but when I see an officer sniff the air and turn in Logan's direction, blind panic fills me.

In an instinctive reaction, I jump from my hiding spot. As I prepare to dart after Logan, to warn him that he's been made, a strong hand clamps down on my shoulder and my legs are kicked out from beneath me. My head cracks the pavement and the world around me goes fuzzy.

I hear a scuffle, then, "Grab her arms."

Blood seeps from my ears and spills across the pavement, the coppery scent mingles with the pounding inside my skull and lets me know I'm still alive. I pry one eye open and as my glance flits over my captors, comprehension slowly sinks in.

Despite the fact that I'm outnumbered, my survival instincts surge and force me to react. Since I'm unable to run, I know I have to fight because my wolf, intimidated by no one, refuses to be taken down by these PTF officers. Especially after having come so far.

But as I'm dragged deeper into the alley by two hard men who've been trained to shoot first and ask questions later, I can't help but fear the worst.

With desperation fueling me on and knowing my only chance at survival is to shift, my clothes tear and I call on my primal side. A ferocious howl rips from my throat and sends the men into action.

"Quick, subdue her before she finishes," one cop yells out to the other two as his hand hovers over his gun. "Our orders are to bring her back to the estate alive. If she shifts I'll have to shoot her."

I hurry to morph, the pain pulling my focus to the point of distraction, but I don't miss the significance in what he's saying.

The PTF are working for my master!

My incisors puncture my gums and moments before I'm about to go feral, I see one man pull a needle from his pocket. I growl and try to break the hold the other two have over me.

With my transformation incomplete, I kick, claw and bite

at the officers as they hold me down. But when a needle jabs my neck and I feel a cold, syrupy fluid pump into my body—a fluid I can only assume is liquid silver—it begins to slow me down.

I give a broken gasp and lash out at the man knelt beside me, refusing to go down so easily. As he scuttles backward, fury obscures my vision and red dots dance before my eyes. But when some small coherent part reminds me that they want me alive I know I still have a fighting chance.

And that's good enough for me.

I blink my mind into focus and work to push past the nausea welling up inside me. I wipe the blur from my eyes and assess my odds as I glare at the three men surrounding me.

Feeling both mentally and physically sluggish, I roll onto my stomach and try to crawl to the street. With my brain barely functioning the best plan I can come up with is to make it to the open so I can scream for help. If people come running, perhaps I can escape under the cover of the commotion.

The men don't move. Instead they all rise to their feet and stand there like storefront mannequins, watching over me like they're waiting for something to happen. The skin on my knees and elbows tear as I drag my body across the hot, black pavement, but when someone steps in front of me and blocks my exit, a cry lodges in my throat.

Stone!

I open my mouth to say his name, to tell him to run, to save himself, but my tongue is so thick I can't speak. I try to reach him telepathically, but I'm unable to sort through the confusion in my brain long enough to articulate a clear thought.

The officer hovering beside me turns to see Stone and the world around me tilts. Because in two seconds flat I know they'll knock the alpha wolf to the ground right alongside me. I can't let that happen. I can't let Stone die because of me.

Except when they all exchange a knowing look, and Stone takes a stand beside the officer, I diligently try to shake the fog from my head and figure out what's going on.

The cop gestures with a nod and hands Stone a thick rope. "Secure her legs."

My fuzzy glance goes from Stone to the cop back to Stone again and I can hardly believe what I'm hearing. Struggling to pull the veil back on my drug induced mind, I try to scurry away but Stone drops to the ground and grabs my ankles.

"*Pride?*"

As he pushes his way into my rattled thoughts I can feel his tension, his worry.

"*Can you hear me?*"

It's then that I realize he's speaking to me privately, his words meant for me and me alone. As he fiddles with the rope, I listen to his blood pound hard.

Guarded eyes meet mine and give a warning. "*Don't let them know I'm with you.*"

I breathe deep and that when I taste his fear, as thick in the air as the stench of the dumpster behind me. It settles on the back of my tongue and has my alarm bells jangling.

Stone is afraid.

"*I need you to shift, Pride,*" he demands as he restrains my legs. "*It's the only way you can fight this.*"

I force my head up and when I see a flash of possessiveness in his eyes, it occurs to me just how wrong I've been about him. Heartache sets my chest on fire and my insides tighten to the point of pain. I close my eyes against the flood of emotion as the truth unfolds before me.

Stone is on my side.

He's always been on my side.

And all this time he hasn't just been watching me. He's

been watching over me.

"*We don't have much time. Do it now.*"

I struggle to morph but as pain erupts inside my weakened body my wolf rebels, completely incapacitated by the poison flowing through my veins.

I lower my head. "*I can't,*" I manage to choke out.

"*You can and you will.*"

I glance at him, my throat aching painfully. "*Stone...*"

His eyes go dark when he says, "*So that's it then, kitty-cat? After everything you've been though you're just going to roll over and die?*" He makes a tsking sound. "*So weak.*"

"*I am not weak!*" I scream back.

He smirks at me and under the guise of leashing me, he continues to wrap the rope around my legs. I growl up at him and much to my surprise my canines punch through my gums.

Stone looks at my fangs and jeers, "*Come on kitty-cat, I thought you had more in you than that.*" Blood pounds in my ears as I listen to him mock me. "*It's not much wonder these guys caught you. Clearly the master made a mistake in sending out a pup like you.*"

As he taunts me it adds fuel to the fire brewing in my stomach. Hating for anyone to see a weakness in me, I embrace my fury and use it to feed my wolf. My nostrils flare, my blood pumps faster, and my nails begin to extend.

Pewter dances in his eyes as he coaxes me. "*That's it, kitty-cat.*"

I feel myself growing stronger and when the fog in my brain begins to dissipate I become aware of what he's doing. He wants me angry. Provoking me the best way he knows how—by using my biggest fears against me. It's my anger that feeds my primal side and the only thing that can nullify the effect of the drug is my wolf's regenerative abilities.

As my blood pushes the poison through my body, I see a flash in the distance and look past Stone's shoulders. When I narrow my eyes, I see Logan. But when Logan shakes his head and turns his back on me, the world around me begins to fade.

I hear a bark of laughter from one of the officers. "Looks like your boyfriend over there is more interested in saving his own ass than yours."

As the alley sways, drifting in and out of existence I watch Logan round a corner. In that instant, every old fear I have comes rushing back to the surface.

Is the officer right?

Is Logan a wolf who'd save himself in the face of danger, like I first feared?

My nails grow longer as I catch one last glimpse of Logan before he disappears from my sight.

The old Pride, the one who thought with her head and not her heart, would have instantly second-guessed Logan's intentions, would have assumed he is out to save himself.

But this Pride, the one who's been through a lifetime of changes over the last few days and is learning to fight with her heart as well as her head knows better than to second-guess the alpha who has always come through for her.

Once again I think about what my mother said, trust no one but family. And that's exactly what I'm going to do.

Because Logan is family.

The officer gives me a cruel grin, nods to his partner and says, "Go get him."

No!

In that instant, as I think about them hurting Logan, or even Stone, rage races faster through my blood and clears the last of the poison. As the chaos in my mind comes to a screeching halt, a low growl rumbles deep in my throat.

When my glance locks with Stone's and I see the upward curve of his mouth, it tells me that he knows.

He knows I'm back.

16

"What the—"

Before the officer can get the words out, both Stone and I morph. Our clothes rip and the sound pulls the attention of the other officers.

Guns are drawn as we square off—outnumbered by one—but when Logan jumps from the rooftop and takes two officers down with him, his presence evens the odds.

As their guns skid across the pavement, Stone lets loose a ferocious howl and pounces, joining Logan in the fight. Before the last cop standing can get a shot off, I leap through the air and knock him to the ground.

Letting wolf instincts guide me I go for his throat. My teeth puncture salty flesh and I want to cry with joy as the coppery taste of his blood slides over my tongue. That first delicious taste has my wolf wailing, delirious with want. She lets loose a deep guttural howl and revels in the pungent tang of his sweet nectar.

Hunger prowls through me as I press on his chest with my paw and sink my teeth in further, searching for his jugular. My wolf gives a little yelp, anxious to puncture the blood-filled vein, to feel the rich warm blood rush into her mouth.

He's yelling something, but I can't make out what he's saying. His hands push at me, eager to gain leverage so he can go for his gun, but I'm too strong. Savage growls fill the air beside me and I can hear both Stone and Logan trying to reach me.

But I'm too distracted. To distracted by the beautiful, aromatic scent of blood as it saturates the alleyway. I breathe deep, pulling the fragrance into my lungs to savor, but then suddenly another smell seeps past the hunger and does something to me.

Something that reminds me I'm not a cold-blooded killer.

As the smell of death surrounds me it's all I can do not to weep as I look at the man beneath me. I take note of the fear in his eyes, the white pallor of his skin, the unnatural twist of his neck and I begin wonder, is he any different than me?

Is he not just doing what he's been trained to do? Just like my wolf is doing what she's been trained to do?

But since I've left the compound haven't I've been taught to control my primal side, taught that I'm more than just a killing machine?

Perhaps these men could benefit from learning a thing or two as well, mainly that not all wolves are cold-blooded killers like they believe.

If I kill him now, wouldn't I simply be feeding into that belief? That last thought stops me cold and I breathe deep to take control of my ravenous wolf.

As her hackles settle, only one thought fills me. The killing has to stop.

I tear my mouth from his neck, and toss my head to the side to see the others. Both Logan and Stone are watching me. I look at the officers trapped beneath them. When I see that they're wounded, not dead, I inch back and do a quick assessment of the man I'd taken down. He's lost a lot of blood, but from the confusion on his face I know he's still alive.

I shake off my wolf and as we all morph back Stone and Logan take up position on either side of me. Breathing hard, silence stretches as I search for my clothes.

"*Are you okay?*"

I turn to Stone as he speaks to me telepathically in his human form and I could sob at the pain I see in his eyes. "*Yes, are you?*"

When he nods, I twist around to check on Logan. He's staring at me, an odd look on his face.

I touch his cheek, concerned. "Are you okay?" I ask, unable to use telepathy with him.

He nods and gestures toward the fire escape staircase leading to the top of the building. "Stay right here. I need to get my clothes. Then I'll be right back."

"Okay."

I twist back around, but when I do, I no longer see Stone. Frantic, I rush to the mouth of the alleyway. Caution aside, Stone walks along the sidewalk, toward one of the master's handlers who, undoubtedly, is searching for me. I open my mouth to yell.

Logan clamps his hand over my mouth and hauls me against him. "It's too late," he whispers.

I spin around and rush out, "You don't understand. You don't know what they'll do to him."

"Pride—"

My stomach cramps and I almost forget how to breathe. "He'll be brutally punished. I can't let that happen."

"He's buying you time, Pride."

I steal another quick look at Stone, and can feel a deep sadness seeping from him. Pain slices at my heart to know I'm the one who put it there.

I give a savage shake of my head. "I can't let him."

Logan spins me back around to face him. "Listen to me," he says, worry sharpening his words. "Right now you're not in any position to stop it."

I look at him and while I know he's right, that it will take careful planning to take down my master, it doesn't make it any easier to swallow.

Before I can say anything, before I can tell him of my plan to go back and that I want to ask his family for help, we hear the ferry sound the horn.

"We need to go."

I nod.

"Stay here. I'll get dressed then pull the car around."

Moving numbly, I morph back to wolf. Logan grabs my torn clothes and rushes up the staircase. A moment later he pulls the car up to the alleyway and I jump into the passenger seat beside him. He's speaking to me, but I have no idea what he's saying. When he pats his leg, I curl up on the plush fabric and lay my head on his lap. As he runs his hands over my fur, I snuggle in close and once again put my safety in his hands.

Exhausted, and unable to communicate during the crossing, I take that quiet time to sort through matters and work on a plan to free the others.

A long time later when darkness is upon us Logan negotiates his car off the ferry. He travels along the highway and when the traffic slows he pulls his car over.

I take that time to morph back. "Hey," he says in a soft voice. "I've missed you."

"I've missed you, too," I say as his warmth wraps around my heart.

With that he reaches into the back seat and hands me a t-shirt and pair of sweat pants. "They're big, but they'll do the trick."

After I hurry and dress in Logan's clothes, he pulls back

onto the road. Both lost in our own thoughts we don't talk about what happened, and we definitely don't talk about Stone. Perhaps neither of us is ready for that just yet.

A long while later he drives through a street lined with houses. I sit up and look at all the quaint homes and when I hear children playing on their lawns or passing a puck on the pavement, my heart turns over in my chest.

"We're here," he says as he pulls into a driveway.

I blink up at him, and we exchange a look before I take in the two-story house in front of me.

"Ready?"

I nod but nervousness invades my stomach. Logan comes around to my side of the car and opens the door. He grasps my hand and gives it a reassuring squeeze.

"Don't worry. It's going to be okay."

He leads me up the walkway but the front door swings open before we even reach the landing. We're instantly bombarded by a group of anxious people who are all talking at once and ushering us inside.

It's so overwhelming that I find myself moving closer and closer to Logan. He pulls me in tight and does a quick round of introductions. Everyone is watching me, like they're waiting for some sort of reaction.

Logan senses my distress and leads me down a long hallway and into the sitting room. He guides me to the sofa and sits down next to me as everyone fills in the seats around us. The lady he introduced as his aunt comes in with trays of food and sweets. And all eyes turn on us, anxious to hear about our journey as the food is passed around.

As Logan begins to fill them in on our run, my thoughts return to Stone, Jace, Clover, and the puppies and anxiety wells up inside me.

I look at the people smiling at me, and understand those still trapped at the compound have offered me this life. They wanted me to have my freedom, even at their own expense. A wave of unstable emotions makes me feel light-headed. I'm not about to let them suffer while I lavish. I have to go back. I have to fight. I have to put a stop to the brutality once and for all.

As I look around Logan's pack—a loving family who, without question, have welcomed me with open arms, I know I can't ask them to risk their lives by joining me in my dangerous pursuit against my master. It's my fight and I have to fight it alone.

I have to say goodbye to Logan and I have to do it now before I get in any deeper. I sniff and when I brush at my face, my fingers come away wet.

A hush falls over the room and Logan gestures for everyone to leave. After they all exit the room, he turns to me and pulls me closer.

His voice drops to a whisper, "Are those tears, Pride?"

"No," I say, and give a big hiccupping sob.

"Ah, you're not so tough after all," he teases, trying to lighten my mood as he uses his thumb to brush away the moisture.

"Weren't you the one who said I should never be underestimated?"

He pulls a face and quivers, feigning fear, "Oh, yeah. You're right."

I pound his chest. "Logan, you don't understand."

"Hey, come on." He shackles my wrists and holds them to his chest. Heat and strength radiate from his body and only makes what I have to say harder. "What is it?" he asks.

"I have to go back." Contrary to my words I lean into him and my heart aches so much it feels like it's going to explode. But I know what I have to do, and I'm determined to do it.

Still, it doesn't make leaving Logan, his family, and the chance to live a normal life any easier.

"I have to go," I say again and climb to my feet.

"I know you do, Pride." Logan stands and pulls me into him. "I know you have to go."

I swallow and blink up at him. "You do?"

"Of course I do. You're smart, strong and whether you want to admit it or not, you're the most compassionate girl I know."

I sniff and as I force myself to take a step back I work hard to desensitize. "Please say goodbye to your family for me. They seem so—"

Logan shakes his head, pulls me hard against his chest and cuts me off. "Don't you see, Pride. I was waiting for you that night at the pub. Waiting for you to come find me."

My mouth drops open and equal measures of shock and confusion rush through me. "What are you talking about?" I recall our initial meeting and remember those fleeting moments when I felt like he'd known who I was, like he'd been waiting for me.

"Because I needed the smartest wolf in the compound at my side."

"To make it through the woods?" I ask and give a quick shake of my head. "I don't think so. You were the one who kept me alive."

"What I was doing was training you."

I have no idea what he's getting at. I look at him, confused. "For what?"

"You have all the makings of a great hunter, but what you lacked was real life experience. I was there to give it to you. If we're going to retaliate against our masters, we have to be prepared for anything and everything."

I gasp, shocked. "You mean..."

"Yes, I mean we're all going back." He waves to the group of men and women hovering near the door watching us.

"Logan, I don't understand."

"We heard rumors about wolves who were being imprisoned, and my pack sent me to investigate. I allowed myself to be captured on purpose so I could better understand the workings of the system. I broke you out because at the estate where I was held we all heard stories about Pride. Smart, lethal Pride who even the handlers were afraid of. If there was one wolf that could help us break back in, and free the others, I knew it was you."

I shake my head and I try to take it all in. "So you actually wanted the handlers to find you at the pub."

He shivers. "I practically lit myself on fire to be found. What I hadn't expected, however, was for the PTF to show up. Although I shouldn't have been surprised. I'd been running around town in wolf form and causing a load of trouble, hoping to get the attention of our masters. They knew I'd removed my microchip so I knew they'd send their best tracker after me." He grins and taps my nose. "And they did."

"Is that why my master was so angry? Because you figured out how to remove the microchip?"

"I suspect he knows who I am and is worried about a retaliation from my pack. He wanted me stopped before I reached the border, and he wanted me alive so he could interrogate me." He goes quiet for a moment and his voice drops, to showcase the seriousness of the situation. "I believe he knows we're going to come for him, Pride, and that makes our rescue mission much more dangerous."

I realize what he's saying fits in with Stone's theory. The master rewired the estate with a new system not to keep his wolves in, but to keep an army of wolves out.

I lower my voice and ask. "Why have you kept this from me?"

Logan looks past my shoulder, a silent signal to his family and a moment later we're all alone. "I wanted you to come to me on your own terms. I wanted it to be your decision."

"How did you know I would make the right one?"

He grins and the warmth in his expression becomes my undoing. "Because you're a wolf who lives up to her name."

"So it's not because your name is Logan and you're so smart?" I question and eye him skeptically, wanting to get to the bottom of what his name really means.

He grins. "Ah, yes, that." He hugs me and my pulse leaps. "If you must know the truth, Logan means hollow."

My head comes up with a start. "Hollow?"

"Yes, hollow."

I wave my hand around. "Like empty space or air."

"Pretty much," he says.

I laugh. For the first time in my entire life I laugh and as a rich, musical sound fills the air it surprises us both.

"Why didn't you tell me what your name really meant?"

"Would you really have trusted a wolf who was named after empty space?"

"Come on, Logan, there must be more to it than that. Your parents would never have given you a name that was so...undignified."

Logan taps me on the nose a second time and says, "Such an astute little girl. Okay, it also stands for tree hollow," he explains.

When I give him a puzzled look, he continues with, "A tree hollow is a branch or trunk that provides a habitat to others. Like you, I'm a protector. As the alpha, it's my job to oversee the pack and make sure all needs are being met."

We stare at each other for a long, thoughtful moment and I think about how much we've been through over the last few days and how much more we're going to go through in the upcoming weeks, and I can't help but think how happy it makes me to know we're going to go through it together. An invisible band tightens around my heart.

In the span of a few short days my life has been turned

upside down. Since I met Logan I've learned a great deal about myself, and about others. I've learned to trust in myself, to use my size as a strength, and to fight with my heart as well as my head.

But most importantly, I've learned about trust and companionship. Although deep in my heart, I know what I feel for this strong alpha goes much deeper than casual friendship.

My pulse races as I stare at the boy who always believed in me—a boy who has taken me from a strong wolf to an even stronger girl.

"Logan," I murmur under my breath as our glances collide.

He dips his head and wets his mouth and I know he's going to kiss me. "Yes," he whispers in the softest voice.

I part my lips, welcoming his mouth to mine. "I think it's a great name. It suits you."

"So does yours."

As his lips settle firmly on mine, I don't refute because I know Logan is the only wolf—the only boy—who knows me well enough to say that.

Well, with the exception of Stone, maybe.

## AFTERWORD

**Thank You!**

Thank you so much for reading Pride's Run, book one in my Pride series. I hope you enjoyed the story as much as I loved writing it. Please read on for an excerpt of Pride Unleashed, and keep your eyes out for Pride's Pursuit.

Interested in leaving a review? Please do! Reviews help readers connect with books that work for them. I appreciate all reviews, whether positive or negative.

Happy Reading,
   *Cathryn*

The night is thick, dark, and ominous—much like my current disposition. All around me the vineyard's nightlife falls mute, the cacophony of familiar sounds muffled beneath the heavy, menacing mood. Tension hovers overhead like a threatening rain cloud and my flesh tightens, waiting for the sky to crack open and fracture the silent night. Even the crickets stand down, their chorus hushed as they sit watching, waiting, listening for the hammer to fall, or in this case, the silver to pierce.

It unnerves me to think that the nocturnal creatures surrounding the estate—a mansion where I'd once been imprisoned—instinctively know that I, along with the pack of wolves at my back, are walking head first into danger and chances of survival are slim at best.

Not unless I can deceive him. The master. A coldblooded human who kept me under his strict control for seventeen long years. The same man who taught me to trick, to lure, to embrace my primal side in an effort to hunt the ruthless drug dealers who dared to cross him. But I'll have to put on my best performance yet if I want to fool the soulless predator who uses both silver and abuse to dominate his wolves.

And they call me the monster.

The second I surrender and he slaps a collar around my throat, I know what I'll have to do—convince him that I hadn't run away from the compound and had only been following his orders to hunt down a rogue wolf.

But showing no emotion in the face of an enemy who is as cunning as he is powerful might not be as easy as it once was. Not after everything I've been through. The fact that I've changed while running in Olympic National Park with the rogue wolf in question, however, is a point in my favor. The master no longer knows all my weaknesses.

Or any of my strengths.

I angle my head to see Logan, the boy/wolf who wound

himself around my heart and helped me learn so much about the world, and about the girl inside me. When my eyes lock on his, my stomach punches into my throat and I swallow a cry of anguish.

Emotions crowd me because I realize Logan's fate is in my hands and I know what will happen to him once I turn him over to the master. I must abandon him like he's nothing more than a tick on my ruff, like what happened between us in that cave two weeks ago during the full moon was nothing more than a diversionary tactic. Despite our bond, I understand it's the only way we can get inside the fortified compound, the only option we have. But it still doesn't make feeding him to the wolves, so to speak, any easier.

I smile at my new mate but my expression slips when I turn away. The truth is I'm frightened. Frightened for Logan. Frightened for the pack of wolves at our backs, for the pack still trapped inside—what will happen if I can't get them out? And I'm frightened for Stone, the alpha who pretended to be my enemy but who risked his very life to save mine.

I can only hope that the boy I've known since childhood was able to use his wit and resourcefulness to stay alive. But what if I'm wrong? What if the master kills him because of me?

I draw in a sharp breath and work to desensitize. I can't let panic get the better of me. Not now. Not after I've come so far.

Keeping to the shadows and camouflaging ourselves in the hostile night, my footsteps slow as we reach the long winding driveway leading up to my former master's estate. With my sight unhindered by the darkness, I glance past the thick iron gate defending the perimeter and take in the sprawling mansion nestled at the foot of Mount Sirren.

On the south ridge of the mountain, overlooking the estate, fields of grapevines provide a gorgeous backdrop to the majestic manor. As I inhale the familiar scents, I struggle to tame the wolf pacing restlessly inside me, but I can't seem to marshal the unease seeping from my every pore.

Even though our aim is to get in and out as quickly as possible—no one wants to be inside the compound any longer than necessary—it's still a risky plan, dangerous, and the scars marring my body are a constant reminder that disobedience comes with a price. If I make one wrong move, one small mistake under the master's watchful eye, not even the capable alpha beside me or the pack of werewolves who make up our small army will be able to step in and stop him.

Something I long ago vowed to do.

My ears perk for sound, and I note that the propane-fired cannons, a device used to scare birds from the vineyard, are quiet tonight. But come tomorrow they'll blast again. At least they'd better blast, because my plan to get the others out alive hinges upon it.

Floodlights sweep the area, splashing monstrous shadows over the manicured lawns and towering marble sculptures. As I take in the array of statues fringing the walkway I can't help but think they resemble an armed band of soldiers ready to defend the empire, prepared to kill all those who threaten their leader. I look beyond them, and in the distance I spot the front door with its ornate, silver doorknocker.

As I glare at it, my heart thunders and my blood pumps faster. The majestic entranceway might look welcoming to most, but I know it's not. I know the cruelties that await us on the other side. But instead of heeding common sense and running in the opposite direction, we're walking straight back in, simply because it's the only way I can follow through with the vow I once made to myself.

Logan moves closer, sensing my discomfort. Unwilling to give in to my fears, I breathe in his comforting scents, pulling them deep into my lungs. The heady bouquet of clean earth

—a fragrance that reminds me of cool, summer days—mingles with the fresh aroma of pine needles. The aroma seeps under my skin and as it travels through my veins I suddenly can't help but wish I was facing the master alone. I hate the risk Logan is about to take. Hate that he's so sure of me that he's willing to put his life in my hands.

Aware of the security cameras panning the area, I take a tentative step closer to the intercom outside the gate. But fear for Logan's safety has my stomach rebelling as the bulging black button taunts me. I want to reach for it, but I can't seem to move, my mind and body no longer functioning on the same wavelength.

Logan curls his hand around my waist, and I jump at his touch. He slides me a look as those perceptive blue eyes of his slowly move over my face, a careful assessment that makes me uncomfortable.

His voice is low, reassuring and I try not to fidget when he whispers, "It's going to be okay, Pride."

I force a smile and my wolf bristles, but I no longer let her take comfort in his touch, or the warm strength of his body. Right now I need to draw on my anger, because it's that anger that's going to keep my wolf sharp and keep us alive.

"Pride," he says again in that soft tone that always gets to me, then he pauses to add depth to his words when he states, "We've all got your back. Nothing is going to go wrong."

"I know," I respond and study his family as I work to keep my voice from sounding uncertain. Although Logan is smart, strong and skilled, we're no longer playing in his territory. While his world might have dangerous black bears, birds of prey, and wild, feral animals, the king of my jungle is far more deadly.

And we'd be wise to remember that.

With life and death hanging in the balance, a dark shiver pulses in my blood. Ignoring the warning sign, I reach out and stab the security button. My mind takes that time to run through various scenarios. As I wonder how the master will receive us, knowing that the next few minutes will determine our fate, I pull a gun from my back pocket and aim it at Logan's head.

I turn to look at Logan's uncle, Malcolm, the powerful leader of the handpicked group of wolves who make up our motley crew. Since I know very little about each wolf, their strengths and weaknesses, I had zero input into who came and who stayed back to oversee their small Canadian community near the border.

But I do know that those who are with us now have risked their lives to help me free the others and for that I'll always be grateful.

Malcolm gives me a curt nod, bringing my attention back to the crisis at hand, and then his brown eyes take on a serious edge when he looks past my shoulders.

I don't need to turn to know what he's looking at. I can hear the gears grinding on the security camera as it slowly pivots my way. Returning Malcolm's signal with a stiff nod of my own, and summoning every ounce of courage I possess, I watch the team of eight retreat, losing themselves in the inky darkness surrounding the estate.

Once they've disappeared, I draw a fueling breath to clear my thoughts and remember what my father taught me when I was just a pup, before he blew out of my life like a leaf caught in an updraft. Never let them see your fear.

But thoughts of my father have my head spinning and fill me with a million questions. Mainly, could he still be alive?

I square my shoulder and begin to turn, to face the firing squad about to descend upon us, but moments before the camera lands on me, Logan's cousin, Gem steps from the darkness to give me a brisk hug.

"Grasshopper," she whispers into my ear. I instantly

remember Logan once calling me grasshopper, but before I can ask what she means, she's gone, disappearing as quickly as she'd appeared, a bright shiny jewel dimmed by the ebony blackness owning the night.

I shift my focus to Logan and I'm about to question him. I want to ask what Gem means, but I also want to know why Malcolm would bring a spirited, energetic girl like her along—one who would surely collapse in the heat of battle. But he squeezes my arm in a silent message, letting me know it's time to focus.

A look passes between us, and then he lowers his head like a broken puppy—one who was just brutally kicked. My heart misses a beat as I watch him put on his game face and execute our plan to perfection. This strong yet gentle alpha never fails to amaze me and everything about him touches me in places I never knew existed until we met.

But I can't think about that right now, can't think about how he makes me feel so warm and secure when I'm with him. Right now I have to get my head in the game and focus on the task at hand, because once that gate opens we'll be anything but safe.

When I tear my gaze away from the boy who taught me how to trust, I remove all emotion from my face and look pointedly at the metal gate. Once again I remind myself that this risky plan needs to go down without a hitch, otherwise I might not ever feel Logan's warm touch again.

Shivers skitter down my spine at the sound of the oxidized hinges yawning open, yet I keep my face blank, my eyes vacant. Less than a split second later the sound of squealing tires reaches our ears. I brace myself for battle and blink against the glaring headlights aimed our way.

*It appears the firing squad has arrived.*

I peer into the darkened windows of the approaching vehicle and spot Lawrence, one of the handlers who takes pleasure in using a rough hand to restrain the wolves. I pan the inside of the vehicle and note that he's brought two body-guards as backup, the same ones I'd managed to ditch and elude at Olympic Park some three weeks ago.

The bulletproof SUV they're traveling in screeches to a halt just inside the gate. The three slowly emerge from the oversized luxury Blazer, and a crooked yet cautious smile curls Lawrence's thin lips as his dark, beady eyes lock on mine.

"Well, well," he says, as he swirls a metal collar around his index finger. It doesn't go unnoticed by me that he's using the thick, steel plated driver's side door to shield his body. That action speaks volumes and reminds me that while I'm the one they keep caged, he's the one who's truly afraid. "Would you look at what the cat dragged in?"

He exposes ugly stained teeth as his spiteful glance goes from me, to Logan, back to me again. I hold his gaze unflinchingly, fully aware of the two guns pointed at my head. I dart a quick look at the guards who are wielding those weapons, evil men who'd love to pump me full of silver should I make one wrong move.

As I take a moment to size them up my wolf stirs, but I calm her, warning her now is not the time to attack. She'll have her chance soon enough, I remind her.

Soon enough...

Lawrence clicks his tongue and makes a tsking sound as his focus settles on our bedraggled states. Logan's eyes inch up, but I shove my gun into his temple to stop him before he can challenge the handler. His head jerks and he growls deep and I can't quite tell whether he's simply playing along or if we're in real danger of him shifting and attacking.

As a protective wolf, and a boy who never goes down without a fight, I understand it's hard for Logan to let someone mistreat his mate, but the last thing I want him to do is defy the handler. It's much too soon for that.

"Nice and easy, kitty cat," Lawrence says and I hear the slight vibration in his voice when he crooks his finger. "Drop the gun and kick it my way."

I lower my weapon and let it fall to the pavement. It clangs on the ground, the sound puncturing the silence of the night. Using the inside of my foot I kick it toward him, giving a little more force than necessary. Despite having just warned Logan to behave, when it comes provoking Lawrence, I can't seem to help myself. Perhaps it's because of the hateful nicknames he calls me, or perhaps it's because he takes such pleasure in bullying the elders—older wolves who've been beaten and broken. Either way, antagonizing him is worth the wounds that come with disobedience.

The pistol skids past him, and I can feel the strain of Logan's eyes on me, a silent warning. But, just like old times, that little stunt earns me a scowl from the handler and the familiarity of it all helps me regain my focus and concentrate on my next move in this deadly game of cat and mouse.

The bodyguards watch the tense exchange between handler and wolf, and their heads bob back and forth like they're waiting for some sort of signal. Lawrence nods toward the gun and grits his teeth.

"Get it," he orders the man directly behind him, and when the burly guard bends to retrieve the weapon, Lawrence hurls the collar at me, much harder than necessary.

I know he's hoping to catch me off guard, but when I snatch it out of the air with practiced ease, his beady eyes narrow and his lips tighten in annoyance.

Glaring at me, he juts his chin toward Logan. "Leash him up, pet," he says evenly, not wanting me to know how much I've rattled him, but his words belie his emotions. I can smell his anger: hot, gurgling rage bubbling to the surface like a cauldron brimming with decomposing flesh.

The primal side of me howls at the putrid scent and my skin itches in response, my thin flesh burning like a thousand angry bee stings as my wolf cries to break free and go for Lawrence's throat.

Working diligently to fight off the change in the face of my enemy, I turn to Logan. My fingers brush along his neck as I snap the collar around his throat. When his gaze flickers to mine there is nothing I can do to ignore the sick feeling mushrooming in the pit of my gut.

This boy has come to mean so much to me—everything to me—and I can't stomach the thoughts of the abuse he's bound to endure at the hands of my brutal master. Our eyes meet and I can feel him reaching out to me, wrapping himself around my soul in a gesture meant to soothe, calm. Reassure.

"*No. Run!*" A hard, angry voice thunders inside my head, only I quickly realize it's not my voice frantically yelling at me to flee.

Caught by surprise I gasp out loud, my stomach cramping so hard I stagger forward. I clamp my hands over my ears to block the piercing noise, completely unprepared for the violent intrusion.

The sounds of guns cocking quickly pull me back and I struggle to compose myself. Dying now would simply interfere with my mission. And I refuse to let that happen. I take a deep fortifying breath, desperate not to blow our plan.

Knowing what I need to do to regain my focus, I think of my mother, my father, the elders, the puppies, and all the others who were killed or tortured by the master's hands. Anger erupts inside me and I use it to smother the confusion rattling my brain.

Unaware of the voice in my head, Lawrence challenges, "Are we going to do this the hard way or the easy way?"

As Lawrence's question hovers like a loaded bullet, the voice barks again, although this time it's louder and much more insistent. *"Run, Pride! It's not safe for you here."*

Violent, chaotic images flash through my mind and I swallow the saliva coating my tongue, suddenly uncertain as alarm bells jangle, urging me to heed the warning.

*"Stone, don't!"* I bark back. *"It's okay,"* I hurry to explain. *"It's not what you think. I've come with a plan."*

Feeling disoriented, I widen my stance and from my peripheral vision I catch the way Logan is watching me, his blue eyes darkening in distress as they lock on mine. That's when it occurs to me that he knows.

He knows Stone is in my head. Connecting with me in a way my own mate can't.

I shake the buzz from my brain to clear it and that's when I realize what this all means. Stone is alive! He hadn't been killed by the master because I ran away and he failed to bring me back. I'd spent the last couple weeks agonizing over his safety, knowing I couldn't bear it if anything happened to him because of me. I exhale a relieved breath and inside my wolf wails with joy at that small, unexpected surprise. Not only am I ecstatic to learn that Stone is alive, we can use all the help we can get to pull off our risky plan.

As I focus in on Logan and take in the dark, troubled shadows beneath his eyes I can't help but feel an odd sense of betrayal for allowing another alpha into my thoughts. But it's not my fault that Stone and I defy nature and can mentally communicate when in human form. I realize it's not something the other wolves can do, and I can't explain why the two of us are an exception to the rule. All I know is that we are.

"Well," Lawrence probes as he tosses me another leash, the air between us crackling with volatile electricity as he waits for my answer. "Is it the hard way or the easy way, kitten?" he asks again.

With no choice but to block Stone from my thoughts so I can fully concentrate on this current crisis, I catch the collar with a hand that bears deep purple scars—whip wounds received from doing things the hard way. But lessons learned have taught me when to push and when to back off.

Without averting my gaze in a show of submission like I'm supposed to, I continue to glare at Lawrence. After all, the handler wouldn't expect anything less from me. The cold metal collar sends chills scurrying down my spine as I secure the restraint around my neck and snap it in place, my compliance answering his question.

When metal grinds metal, the lock sliding home, Lawrence visibly relaxes because he knows once I'm leashed, shifting is impossible. Not unless I want to put breaking my neck at the top of my to-do list. And right now those top spots are reserved for a select few.

Lawrence steps away from the vehicle and I can't help but bare my teeth as he hooks a heavy chain to my collar and gives it a good hard tug. I jerk forward, my neck nearly snapping like a dry twig, and I can feel Logan's tension spreading like an unleashed virus.

Before it infects Lawrence and causes him to react, I want to tell Logan to back down. We can't break cover, or let the handlers or anyone else in the compound know what we mean to each other. In this prison our feelings for one another will simply be used against us.

I slant my head to see my mate but no matter how hard I try I still can't speak to him telepathically when in human form. Using my eyes, I telegraph a message, and he correctly interprets the meaning. When he lowers his head in submission, I turn back to Lawrence and see the suspicion darkening his eyes.

"Should we get this over with?" I ask in an effort to take his focus off Logan.

There is a dangerous edge to Lawrence's voice, one I've never heard before when he focuses back in on me and says, "Over with? Oh no, Pride, this is far from over." The malicious look on his face tells me he knows something I don't and ribbons of fear trickle along the back of my neck when he adds, "For you, kitty cat, this is just the beginning."

## ABOUT CAT

*New York Times* and *USA today* Bestselling author, Cathryn Fox/Cat Kalen is a wife, mom, sister, daughter, and friend. She loves dogs, sunny weather, anything chocolate (she never says no to a brownie) pizza and red wine. She has two teenagers who keep her busy with their never ending activities, and a husband who is convinced he can turn her into a mixed martial arts fan. Cathryn can never find balance in her life, is always trying to find time to go to the gym, can never keep up with emails, Facebook or Twitter and tries to write page-turning books that her readers will love.

Connect with Cathryn:
Newsletter
https://app.mailerlite.com/webforms/landing/c1f8n1
Twitter: https://twitter.com/writercatfox
Facebook:
https://www.facebook.com/AuthorCathrynFox?ref=hl
Blog: http://cathrynfox.com/blog/
Goodreads:
https://www.goodreads.com/author/show/91799.Cathryn_Fox

Pinterest http://www.pinterest.com/catkalen/